THE HEALING HEART

By: A. L. Whyte

Cover artwork by,
Jason Avery

ISBN: 979-8-9996721-4-8

The Healing Heart is a fictional story based on real events. It discusses serious issues about severe child abuse and suicide. There are potential triggers throughout the story. If anyone should feel triggered, please note that there are state and federal organizations that exist to help. There is a national suicide hotline that you can call or text 988 for help or support. There is also the website, neverabother.org. Here in California, there is the Department of Human Services crisis hotline, 707-445-7715. There is also the website, livebeyondca.org. If you need help, please seek it. You can use any of the above live or website sources. They can also help you find a professional therapist.

You are not alone.

There may be some questions about Eye Movement Desensitization and Reprocessing (EMDR). One of the sites I used during research is EMDR.com. It is home to the EMDR Institute, founded by Francine Shapiro, Ph.D. As the site states, Dr. Shapiro is the originator and developer of EMDR.

Because I chose to write in a fiction format, outside of immediate family, any resemblance to anyone else is coincidental.

ACKNOWLEDGEMENTS

I would like to thank my sweet partner, Kristin, for her input and editing. In addition, I am especially grateful for the technical input and suggestions by Rosy Provino LCSW. Finally, I want to give a big thank you and acknowledgement to my main editor, Amara. She has been invaluable.

While much of this novel is based on true events, I chose to write it as a bio-fiction so I could weave more of these events into one story.

This novel is dedicated to my brother, Kevin.

Baby Lollipops

He should have felt the cool breeze
pushing back his hair on a merry-go-round,
the sky spinning among the trees,
or a kitten,
or another hand, his size, clutching him
in glee.
He should have done so much more.
If he had lived...
He died at three,
tattered and thrown into the weeds.
A little life from a dark place;
shattered because he was hungry;
battered because he cried;
stuffed in a dark closet of fear.
His life slowly ebbed through the holes
in his clothes and his soul.
He must have had that final cry.
A cry for help that could not stop
till the stern hand of punishment
gave him peace of death.
A pitiful cry for help
To those who could not hear...
Rest in peace, Baby Lollipops...
Heaven is a place of tears.

CHAPTER ONE

“That was the night my brother found his roommate’s gun, put it in his mouth and shot himself.” Mike said, allowing the gravity of his words to resonate. He looked out at the attendees of this seminar on Adverse Childhood Experiences (ACEs), who, by being here, were committed to continuing their healing journey. Some pursed their lips, and a few were nodding. It was important to maintain honesty, as anything less would obviously be deceitful. They were acutely aware that much of their lives were shrouded in falsehoods, including the lies they had perpetrated on themselves. Many of them, by now, could easily discern bullshit.

Still, adults affected by ACEs can be overly trusting and have a need for validation, or a need to be liked. Survivors of abuse often carry a certain degree of naivety, perhaps due to their early childhood innocence being ripped away. This desire to reclaim their innocence and their lost trust makes them cautious and even fearful of figures of perceived authority. Yet, they were here to continue their work and hopefully overcome their experience of childhood abuse and, as in so many cases, their self-abuse.

“Some of you can relate to my loss: Some of you have probably attempted to take your own lives; many of you have gone through your life trying to do whatever it takes to numb the pain, the deep insecurity, and in some cases, the shame and the anger and the hate. All of which can lead to toxic stress responses. I know I did. In my late teens and early twenties, I was known as the guy with no personality. I was terrified of being myself; of the truth being discovered that all the abuse must have been my fault. If I did slip and one of my peers told me I was acting weird, whether it was just being a kid or not, I would immediately stifle myself.

"I finally understood that I was deeply afraid that they would know that I was to blame, that I was bad, that I was deeply ashamed. You remember that feeling as a kid or young adult? I know you do. I would use drugs or alcohol to numb the fear, the shame, the pain of being myself, and of the bad memories and nightmares.

"I didn't last long in a relationship because I was afraid my partner would someday discover what I had done. How bad I was. Which, of course, I wasn't. It was my distorted belief that I didn't deserve love. Because of that misguided self-perception, in certain situations I would go numb. Because of the fear of being discovered, sometimes I couldn't even speak. Every part of my life was affected by that form of self-sabotage, including my relationships. Many of you know what I mean. We carried that feeling of guilt and shame and pain into our adulthood. After all, why would the people that took care of us as kids want to hurt us? Obviously, because we were bad. At least, as little children, that's what we told ourselves. Why else would the people who are supposed to take care of you, love you, want to hurt and horribly abuse you. Again, obviously, to us little ones, it must've been our fault. Yet, I promise you, it never was!" Mike stopped to let what he said fall on the people here. He heard some sniffing, and someone was quietly sobbing. It was time to finish this seminar.

"I'm going to end this gathering by retelling a story I heard at a commencement ceremony. A professor recalled an experience she had, that I have never forgotten. She lived along the coast in a rural area of Northern California and was travelling home one evening after an event. Imagine lots of trees and a few houses. An area where the roads meander around the coastal ridges and are not well lit, if at all. She was driving on such a road when she saw a young woman, an ex-student, stumbling along the side of the road. She stopped and asked the girl if she needed a ride home. The young woman said, 'No, I have to do this.' 'Do what?' the prof asked. 'This.' Still not knowing what the clearly inebriated girl was talking about, the professor pleaded with the girl to get into the car. She refused. The professor noted as she prodded the young woman, that she grew increasingly sad and near tears. Finally, seeing that the girl was not going to get into the car and with much regret, the professor got ready to leave. Then she felt a need to say one more thing, and she said, 'I love you.' The girl burst into bitter tears and said, 'I love you too.' Still unmoved, and crying, the girl walked back in the opposite direction. Saddened, the professor reluctantly got back into her car and drove away. The next day the professor heard on the radio of a girl that had lain down in the road and was accidently killed by a young man in a pick-up truck. She investigated and it was indeed the girl she had seen on the road that night before.

"I tell this story because it's based on an actual event. I have taken some license with the telling of this tragedy, but not much. I say this to you because I believe you desire to take back the part of your life that was stolen from you. That part that was abused by the people who should have been there to protect you when you were a child. The part you have kept numb for so long. That omnipresent feeling that 'something is wrong.' Those feelings in a social situation that scream at you, 'This is awkward. I need to leave!' Common enough for most people, but for us abused adults, those feelings also come with a fear, sometimes a deep fear of being exposed. Of what? Our secret abusive past? Secrets! I say no to secrets. Damaged though I may be I will no longer allow the past to dictate how I live in the present, or future.

"I hope you may be able to find a way to do the same. To expunge. I know. As I said, I share the same story of Adverse Childhood Experiences, or ACEs. I am here to tell you that there is a light at the end of the tunnel. I have taken, and when necessary, continue to utilize the same type of therapies you may have experienced. The most important thing that I learned from my evolution is you must learn to love yourself.

"That young girl needed to be loved. As many of us have felt, at one time or another, love was not to be found. And self-love . . . Somewhere someone had told her or by abuse showed her that she was not worthy of loving herself; maybe not even worthy of accepting and being loved.

"The great psychiatrist, Robert Jay Lifton, was asked in an interview by the journalist, Joanne Silberner from NPR, 'You've spent a large part of your life listening to very difficult stories and writing about them. Has this focus on the worst mankind has to offer taken a toll on you?' And he answered, and I'll summarize, 'Yes, I've found I need to have alternative involvements and that includes a lot of love and close relations with one's family and close friends. It also includes diversions.' Well, my such diversion is writing – and rooting for the Miami Dolphins." Somebody in the room laughed, which made Mike laugh. "Yes, a frustrating endeavor for many years, but there is always hope. Mr. R J Lifton was expressing what we all need, and that is to rediscover the love that was stolen from us when we were children. And that's what I wish for all of you to find."

Mike looked about the room. They were all quietly listening, some nodding. Many of them were wiping away tears. They looked like the South Bay community, different ages, colors, sexes, and economics. Yet, they were all peers of a similar unfortunate experience. Sadly, child abusers were represented in every aspect of every society. The people a child looked up to for protection were its parents, and many had failed. Mike continued to speak.

"Please know you are loved. Everybody in this room has empathy and all of you must help each other. You are here because you all have made a choice to say, 'No' to the ghosts of the past. You are here because you all choose to say 'No' to a dismal and self-loathing future. Know that there is hope. Know that you are all worthy of love. Know that you are not alone. With that I wish to thank you and commend you for being here. I am available, on the floor, for a short time. Again, thank you."

Mike left the podium to a polite and subdued applause and walked down the stage stairs toward the audience. Already people were moving toward him. He knew how much pain was in this room. That's why they were here. That's why he was here. He also knew that maybe, at best, fifty percent of the people in this room would find a place of peace that they could live in. They were here because of the pain they suffered, as adults, from the abuses they had endured as a child, from their ACEs. He also knew, from experience, that there was hope. He mentally prepared himself.

The first to approach was a young woman. It made him sad that so many women, no matter their age, were abused by their family: their fathers, their uncles, for God's sake, their grandfathers and others; not to minimize the same horrible abuses to the young men. It just made him sad. For some reason this was an extra sad day for him. It had been through the last few seminars. Still, he greeted them with a positive attitude.

They all had, as they always do, a tearful story to share. Mike reminded them that he was not a therapist but, like them, a reluctant member of the same sad family history. Through his self-help books and seminars, he was there to share the same message he had seen help so many others, as well as himself: "learn to love yourself", meaning learn to love who you are. Find the ability to joyfully be your authentic self, whether in a crowded room, or sitting alone on a mountaintop.

A surprisingly tough road to travel for many humans, but especially those that were abused as children. Because of that he tried to encourage those who were not in therapy to please get back into it. Like the great psychiatrist Dr. Bessel van der Kolk said in the title of his brilliant book, "The Body Keeps the Score", and as he writes in the book, "The brain may keep sending signals to the body to escape a threat that no longer exists."

Because of ACEs, especially sexual abuse, that threat was still there conflicting the brain. Many of the people in Mike's seminars were on a healing path that still needed support. The threat might no longer exist, but the helpless child was still there. Mike encouraged therapy so those affected by ACEs could break the cycle of the dark feeling of some ubiquitous threat, the fear, self-loathing, and self-hate, for something that was never their fault. It often left him drained.

He noticed as the gathering dissipated a young woman, maybe in her thirties, standing back, but looking at him with great sadness. He approached her and asked, "Are you all right?"

"Hi Mr. Smith. I was at your seminar last week in Hayward. I'm having a real tough time," she replied as tears dribbled down her cheek.

"Do you need help? Are you safe?"

"I am, I think, but I just left an abusive relationship and the man I escaped from still has my two children."

"In California, under Child Protective Services, or CPS, there is the Children and Family Services Division. They are very effective in helping people in your situation. I have contact information. Would you like it?"

"I have talked with them. They are trying to help. He has a wealthy family and so far, they have stopped me from rescuing my children. Even though the children have told the judge that they do not want to be with him. He just wants to hurt me. I thought I escaped this male-induced fear from my childhood. He's the same as my abusive father." Tears started to stream down her cheeks.

"Adverse Childhood Experiences are real and lifelong, don't give up."

"Yes, I understand. That's why I am here to see you again. I appreciate your books and positive outlook, very much. I have lived and experienced ACEs. Clearly, as have you, but, right now, it feels hopeless."

"Do you have a therapist?"

"Yes, he's good, but it feels . . . hopeless."

"I'm concerned. You do know about the suicide hotline, 988?"

"Yes, we've talked."

"Please, please, use it."

"I have. I just wanted to talk to you. To thank you." She gave him a small hug and started to walk away. Mike touched her shoulder. She turned toward him and said, "Sorry, I'll be fine."

"Follow your heart. Stick with what you think is right."

"With what I think is right. Yes . . ." Then she left.

Still reeling from that conversation, he headed back to his hotel in the South Bay. Tomorrow, he planned to head back to

Sonoma County and get ready for a family reunion. His daughter had a dog that was getting older, and she wanted to take him back to the house where they had spent a great deal of their youth. The house was the main building on a forty-acre lot near Lake Sonoma. When Mike and his wife divorced, they sold their home. It was a place where the two girls had fond memories, and the present owners were using it as an Airbnb. Mike had secured it for a weekend, three weeks from now. He was looking forward to a big family gathering.

He dropped his seminar books and papers on the bed. He took some time to settle his mind and aimlessly scanned different stations on the hotel TV. He wasn't really watching. It was a distracting form of meditation. The young mom's conversation from earlier kept circling his brain. Finally, he decided to head down to the hotel restaurant. He ordered a meal. He was glancing at his phone when he heard someone pull a chair out and sit at his table. He looked up and saw a man who was clearly a detective from the badge on his jacket.

"Are you Mike Smith?" He asked.

"Yes, sir. What can I do for you?"

"Did you have a conversation or meeting or interaction with an Elizabeth Carrington recently?"

"I don't know that name. Why, officer?"

"Do you recognize this woman?" The detective showed a picture to Mike. A terrible empty feeling ran through his gut.

"I do, officer. We spoke briefly at the end of my seminar earlier this afternoon." Mike looked up at the detective and with a certain amount of fear asked, "Why?"

"I am sorry to say she took her own life late this afternoon. She left an extensive note, but at the end she said, 'Tell Mr. Smith I did the right thing.'"

"Oh, no..." Mike sank into his chair closed his eyes and near tears, again said, "No..."

"I'm sorry Mr. Smith. I can see you're distraught. I had to talk with you about this to close the case. I'm deeply sorry." Mike couldn't find it in him to acknowledge the officer. The detective again said, "I'm very sorry," and got up and left. Mike, stunned, just stared.

"Sir, your food." The waiter stood patiently near the table with a dish in his hand.

"I've lost my appetite."

"Shall I make it to go?"

Mike stood, clearly in pain, and looked at the waiter. He gave him two twenty-dollar bills. "You have it, please."

"Do you need some help, sir?" The waiter looked concerned.

"I just need to go lay down." He turned to leave.

"God bless you, sir."

Mike just wanted to scream, but he knew that the waiter's words came from a place of kindness. He looked at the waiter and gave a very small nod and left to go to his room.

He worked himself into bed and let the tears flow as they would. That night his nightmares returned.

> The child was pushed down, face first, over a bed or something. He didn't know. All he knew was that he had no power. He wanted to scream but all that came out were pleas, and there was punishment if he protested too much or was too loud. So, he kept the screams internal. Even so, he still bleated in pitiful pouts mixed with fear and the question, "Why?" Who held him down? He couldn't see. Somewhere there were adults who were supposed to protect him. Still, any questions of protection were confusing because those adults were in the nightmare. Someone held him down. An infinitely dark blanket rushed toward his head. He finally succumbed to a scream. The dark blanket covered his head as he screamed in his little boy voice. Then a smash cut, as dreams do, and he was a tiny human hiding under a piece of furniture. His father was yelling and hitting his mom. He grabbed her and pushed/threw her across the kitchen floor. She began crawl-

ing along the floor, turned red by the cuts on her knees as he ran at her again. The tiny child, his hands in the air, palms out, screamed and cried for his father to stop.

Mike's own little boy screams woke him up. He ran his hands across his face. He shifted away from the wet pillowcase and the damp, sweat-filled sheets where he had laid during his nightmare. He looked at the hotel's LED clock. It was nearly four in the morning. He pulled himself up and sat on the edge of the bed. It had been years since he'd had these dark dreams. Why now? Though in is healing heart, he knew.

He once had been in that poor woman Elizabeth's state of mind: his brother's state of mind. Yes, he had been abused. Yes, he felt the pain. But he also believed he had left much of it behind. Till tonight. The dreams were almost always the same; the crying child, the deep dark pressure, like a blanket, pushing him down, covering his eyes, the complete helplessness, the inability to move. Still, he had learned, through good therapy, how to become an adult in these horrible nightmares. But tonight, he was unable to change into that adult. Why . . .?

Yet, he knew that the young woman's suicide had brought back, had triggered that secret buried part of his mind, the tortured, abused child that had been part of him for so many years. Triggers can happen at any time. Also, for some reason, the last few seminars had been very difficult and now, culminating with the news he had received at dinner, and the nightmare, it all kind of made sense. Does it ever make any sense?

He took a breath. The light from the front balcony of the hotel was peeking around the edges of a closed curtain. The sounds of traffic on the main road just below were gradually getting louder. People were going to their jobs. He looked over to the duffle bag sitting near the door. The bottle of water he'd bought earlier was on the nightstand next to the bed. He thought about having the next few weeks off and the preparations for a family gathering. All that felt normal. He needed normal. That thought made him smile. Still, the nightmare.

All this thinking and the emotional trauma drained him, exhausted him. Again, he looked at the room clock. It was twenty minutes after four. He checked his surroundings one more time and crawled back into bed. He then thought about his kids. Both his girls were grown and were strong and powerful individuals. The youngest, Rose, at twenty-seven, had a sweet little girl, now four years old, and she had just given birth to a little boy. She turned out to be a wonderful mom.

"I'm a grandpa. Never thought I'd say that." It made him smile. "Okay, time to sleep." Then scenes from the nightmare crept back into his mind.

"What did I say during the seminar? If you need help, get it, seek therapy." Mike thought about the profundity of his statement. It wasn't meant to be a casual thought. He knew what he had to do. "I'll contact her tomorrow," he said. With that he finally went to sleep.

CHAPTER TWO

After a light breakfast, Mike started to make his way up the 101 then through The City, to the Golden Gate Bridge and then north. The Bay Area traffic was normal, but it slowed to a crawl around the Market Street area. As he inched his way through that jam, his mind kept going back to the short conversation he had had with Elizabeth. Was there anything else he could have said or done to persuade her to reconsider taking her own life?

"She left behind her kids. Probably with a cruel father that'll tell the kids, 'Your mom was weak, that's why she died.' He'll work to bring them up in his image, just like he probably was raised in his dad's image," Mike said to himself. His phone rang. Mike touched a button on the steering wheel.

"Hi, sweetheart, how are you doing?" It was his daughter Rose.

"Fine, Dad. Just checking-in. Where are you?"

"Still in SF, crawling along in traffic."

"How was this last seminar?"

"It was tough."

"They're all tough."

"Yes, honey, but these last few have been especially hard, don't know why. I look forward to our family time together."

"Do you want to talk? You know I'm a good listener."

"I do know that. Thanks. It's not much different than what I've shared with you before. Well, this time, a little different. A mom, maybe ten years older than you, met me at the end of the seminar. She was in deep despair because she was losing, through divorce, her two children to a man that couldn't care less about her or their kids. He's just one of those who must win, if you know what I mean. She was incredibly sad. I tried to console her." At the last statement Mike was barely able to speak.

"Oh, Dad. . ." Rose said understanding what may have happened.

"Yeah, she took her life. She was abused by her father, and, like many, she ended up in an abusive relationship. Which sadly reminds me that there are many abused men that grow up and end up being worse than their abusers. Just like the kid I saw years ago at a ballpark. He couldn't have been more than ten. He was walking alongside his dad, who was popping a baseball up and down in his mitt. The boy, obviously excited about being at the game, reached up to try and catch his dad's baseball. The dad backhanded the boy across his face so hard that the kid lost his balance and banged his head, hard on a concrete post. You know, the posts where they park cars. There were no tears.

"The dad quickly looked around to see if anyone noticed his cruelty. Satisfied, he started walking and tossing the ball again, leaving his son behind. The boy looked at his dad, adjusted his glasses, ran to catch-up and happily started to pat his hand into his kid's glove, just like he was doing before his dad brutally smacked him. It was like, 'This is normal, I get beat for nothing all the time'. The kid smiled at his dad. I hope that abusive father dies alone. He deserves nothing less.

"I published a poem years ago called, 'Just Like Him'. It was about that incident. And, I hope, with all my heart, that boy didn't grow up to be like his dad."

"Geez, Dad, you're bringing me way down."

That made Mike smile. "Thanks, daughter, sorry. You do always make me smile. I should be back in Santa Rosa in about two hours give or take, because of traffic. When are we meeting?"

"Well, Sarah and I will be in Sonoma County over the next few days. Tyler and I are staying at an Airbnb till we all get together. Sarah has a place where she can stay in Sebastopol. Once we all get settled in, I'll give you a call. Dad, thank you so much. The old boy will be very excited to see the house again."

"Well, he's a beloved dog. It'll be good to see Zeus again, and my granddaughter. And how's that baby boy?"

"He's amazing!"

"Naturally. What is he, four months old now?"

"Darn close, four and a half."

"Well, I am so looking forward to seeing him, and all of you, of course."

"Of course. Okay, we'll talk to you soon. Bye." Rose ended the call.

The flow of traffic picked up a little bit. Mike still had a smile from his conversation with Rose. Yet Elizabeth crept back into his mind. It made him think about his own life.

There was a time around eighteen years ago when all his insecurities, the unknown fears, the shame and the complete confusion about why he was here, along with the abuse of alcohol and drunken ideas of what it meant to be a man, all of it complicated the pain and confusion he felt in his heart. There was much he still had to learn. In normal life, (whatever that means), the answers were there, though still hard, but in Mike's life there were no simple answers, only tortured questions. The questions haunted his brain for many years. The nightmares were constant, strangers sent him into deep paranoia, to him his relationship started looking like a lie, work was nearly impossible as he spiraled into panic attacks. During that dark period, he seriously thought, like his brother, like Elizabeth, and so many others, about taking his own life.

A very good therapist and the thought of leaving his children behind helped him overcome that devastating time. He gradually pieced himself back together. He learned to become an adult in his nightmares. He learned to accept the love his children offered as well as from his family and his close friends. He eventually found a way to learn to live with himself and with the wounded child that was part of his adulthood. He embraced that child and loved and protected it in his nightmares; since those that were supposed to keep the child from harm, the abusers, were also a part of the nightmares.

Gradually he began to accept the ability to exist in his own skin, to recognize his own thoughts. He was able to love and accept who he was as opposed to metastasizing another human's flawed personality. He no longer was an extension of someone else. He grew to be quite comfortable with his imperfections, his past, and simply being himself. From that growth Mike created a series of books that he hoped would help the many like him find their own path to a positive, emotionally secure and safe life.

Still, it wasn't easy. As he drove over the Golden Gate Bridge, the sheer beauty of the day and the hills drew tears to his eyes. He was easily brought to tears. His daughters often made fun of him, especially when they were all watching a sweet TV show or one of those effective commercials showing a family with joyful, loved children.

"Yep, there goes Dad." They would playfully joke as Mike swelled with empathy.

Perhaps it's because it was one of those things that was ripped away or was absent from my childhood, that sweet love from parents who really do care. Maybe when I see that; the happy child and loving mom, maybe when I see that I miss it and am overwhelmed with a sense of loss, a loss of innocence. Yet, it fills me with deep joy, a flood of empathy, at seeing that loved child.

Mike thought about that and then yelled to no one, "Who knows! I sure don't!"

Then that got him to think about when he left home at seventeen. He had buried deep in his mind much of the trauma he had experienced when he was a little boy. Yet he knew and felt the shame and pain, fear and the PTSD that the abusive experience had caused. In the back of his mind, he was constantly consumed and fearful about a threat, no longer there, yet it still gnawed at his insides.

He knew there was something terribly wrong within the house where he had lived. As soon as he could he left that environment. He constantly fought with his stepfather, one of the main abusers. At least twice it moved to fists. For the sake of his mind and his soul, he couldn't live there anymore. His two younger sisters years later told him he was their buffer, and they wished he'd never left. Something he still carries as guilt, leaving his siblings behind. His brother Kevin tried to intervene but was beaten and abused. When their stepfather was on his deathbed, Kevin screamed, cussed and yelled at him. "I hope you rot in hell," was the last thing he had said before he walked out of the room.

I remember me and my best friend Shoe found a place for $200 a month each. Everybody called him Shoe because of his last name being Shubert. Man, we could party, but Shoe was always the last one standing and always the first to get a girl. Still, there was a sadness hidden in that young man. Mike took a moment to think about his friend. Years later Shoe drove his car into a highway bridge's abutment. He died instantly. Mike shook his head at that sad memory.

He had made his way over the Golden Gate Bridge and was just passing the Tiburon exit. Depending on the traffic he was less than two hours away.

"Girls, oh man, that was another experience. Lots of beauty and joy and lots of pitfalls and hurt," Mike mumbled to himself. The flow of cars was now smooth and up to speed. Mike thought about his experiences with girls when he was in his teens and early twenties, before he married. He laughed as he thought, *hormones were flying everywhere.*

It was a difficult time. Girls befuddled Mike. Raging hormones and young, healthy, beautiful men and women, all with little or no experience and all filled with desire. It's clear that every community has its own level of social acceptance when it comes to sex. Some very restrictive, some very loose, and most somewhere in the middle. Unfortunately for Mike he had no family experience or mentors to guide him with women. All he had were ACEs and the certainty that what had happened to him was wrong.

Because of that he made a pledge to himself that he would never do anything intentionally to hurt another human. That was how he approached not only his friends, but lovers as well. Still, he made mistakes. Sometimes he was too aggressive and was yelled at or slapped by a woman. He lost a couple of good friends because of that. Lessons learned there. At other times he wasn't aggressive enough. One girl at the end of their date night, said, "You're odd. In a nice way, but odd. I'd rather we just be friends." She wanted him to be more physical, whatever that means. In that way women still confused the heck out of him. He also grew into maturity at the end of the so-called free-love generation. Mike was a young teen as that generation was morphing into Yuppies. The free-love idea was still alive and well in high school and junior colleges. It was a tough time to learn and understand women, especially for a young man with no mentors and a terrible family experience and easily manipulated by his so-called friends and their peer pressure.

I remember once in eighth grade, almost fourteen at the time, I had two girlfriends and got into two fist fights on the same day. And then by the end of the day both girls broke up with me! All my peers thought I was cool. I still don't understand what happened that day. Life is a fucking puzzle, Mike thought to himself. Many of those thoughts and mistakes of his youth still perplexed him.

Near the end of that dark period, when he had contemplated suicide, of his deepest depression, in frustration, he angrily yelled at his number one daughter, Sarah. The family had fallen apart, and his daughter was refusing to talk with him. Desperate, and trying to reconnect with her, he lost his patience. Anger set in because of what he perceived to be her lack of empathy. She then completely shut down. In frustration he asked his ex-wife for help. She told him something that changed the way he would talk to women for the rest of his life. She simply said, "You have no idea how scary a loud angry man's voice sounds to a woman."

I did not. It pains me to think how, with just my voice, I could have hurt any woman, especially my daughter. With guilt, that thought circled around his mind.

Mike never raised his voice at a woman again. Some men, eh, they deserved it, but a woman, from that day forward, never again. After all, in the world according to Mike, it was a man's job, when needed, to protect, to be a safe house, for any woman or a child; not to belittle or dominate anyone with his voice or physically, just because he was stronger. There were times of deep frustration, yes, but he managed to grow and learn, to get to a point where his anger did not rule a conversation. It did change his life. He learned to be a better listener, as opposed to loudly jumping into a conversation with his own, angry, self-righteous profundities. All in all, he was in a good place. Still, there was this sudden nightmares and a dark feeling troubling his inner mind.

He was getting close to Petaluma. Santa Rosa was about forty minutes away, when Elizabeth crept back into his thoughts. That led him to think about his brother. Kevin was thirty-two when he took his own life. He, unfortunately, was one of the ones that did not escape his abusive past. He was involved in gang activities. He was an absent father to infant children here and there around the US. He was deeply wrapped in drug and alcohol abuse. Mike remembered asking Kevin for help on some minor house repairs. Kevin showed up at 10am with a case of some Hard lemonade. By afternoon the case was gone. All consumed by Kevin. He was a lost soul. Mike's sister, Arlene, uncovered a diary from her oldest daughter. In the diary the girl described how her Uncle Kevin constantly harassed and touched her in inappropriate ways when she was younger.

Arlene had received the most severe abuse by their stepfather. She leans on psychotropic drugs to maintain her sanity. Her PTSD was difficult to live with. Still, she survived. When she found out what Kevin had done to her daughter, she became violently angry. They had to be kept separate. Finally, Arlene decided to turn over the diary to the police. Kevin was already on probation. Within that week he took his life.

How I cried my eyes out at the funeral. The pain has never gone away. No matter how lost he was, we were always close. As children we watched out for each other in a terribly abusive home. Mike held that thought. He never forgave himself for not being there when Kevin died by suicide.

Mike thought about the funeral and the service afterward. One of the family abusers was his grandmother. She used to dress as a clown and take her act and sometimes her band to various kids' parties. The drummer in her band ended up being a well-known sex addict and abuser. Later in his life he was murdered. Nobody was ever charged, but he also wasn't missed.

Mike blamed his grandmother along with their stepfather for Kevin's depravity and death. In an unpleasant twist, during the service after the funeral, the grandmother called to talk with Mike's mother. His two sisters initially took the call. Knowing that it was their abusive grandmother they gave the call to Mike.

"I couldn't believe she called in the middle of that ceremony. My mother was talking about positive memories of my brother. The few family members that were there were in tears. I remember taking the phone outside and yelling at my grandmother. I told her to never call here again. I remember her saying that I shouldn't talk to her with such anger. Then I yelled at her, screaming that she was responsible for Kevin's death. She stopped talking. She started weeping. I ended the call and never saw her again. It was a cathartic experience." Mike remembered out loud. The pain of that memory began to overwhelm him. He needed help.

"I'll get settled in and then give Lee a call," he quietly said to himself. Lee was a good friend and therapist. He had known her for over a decade. She would open a spot for him. Even though she was a friend, she was professional. He knew that she was able to separate their friendship and offer good pragmatic advice. It wouldn't be a session, just a chance for him to talk with someone he trusted. She would no doubt advise him to seek independent, professional counseling outside of their friendship.

Mike spent a lot of the drive deep in thought and so, to his surprise, he was suddenly in front of his home. He shook his head as he parked and then made his way into his dwelling. He owned a small house off A Street near Julliard Park. After getting settled he called Lee. She was able to set some time for Friday, three days away, at one o'clock. Feeling good about talking with, and soon to see her, he decided to walk to his favorite restaurant, Sisters, down the street. It was a sunny day in late spring. The prevailing weather was comfortable, mid-seventies with a slight breeze.

It was good to be home and walk around the neighborhood.

Mike loved this spot. The trees were mature and offered lots of shade. There were a few artistic stores and a coffee shop. People were always pleasant. It was a part of the so-called art district of Santa Rosa. It even had its own little side road called Art Alley.

He made his way down to the street corner opposite the restaurant. He looked across the main street to see if any cars were heading his way before he crossed. It looked safe. He stepped down to cross and as he did, he saw this man, on the other side of the street looking and pointing at him. For some reason that startled Mike. The man was dressed in white, and he clearly was pointing at Mike, as if he was trying to say something. Mike was frozen as he looked at the man. The man lowered his finger but still stared. Then he raised both his hands and opened his mouth as if to speak. Mike leaned slightly as if to listen. Just then a car's horn blared at Mike. He looked in the direction of the noise.

"What are you doing? Are you gonna cross or not!" The driver was irritable. Rightly so. Mike was standing like a statue just at the edge of the road on the downslope corner of the sidewalk. He looked at the driver, "I am so sorry. Please, you go." He waved the driver on as he backed up the sidewalk. "Really sorry," he said again as the car passed. Remembering the encounter with the man in white, he quickly looked up. The man was gone.

Mike again checked for traffic and hurried across the street. He looked in all directions. The man in white was nowhere to be seen. He went into the restaurant to see if he was in there. He was not. Mike ran outside to look one more time. There was no sign of him anywhere. *Did I even see him?* Mike held that thought for a minute, and then, *Great! Am I now hallucinating?* As he stood staring down A Street, he felt numb. That old feeling of panic began to spin around his torso. "Okay, a glass of wine would be good." He said to himself as he walked into the restaurant.

CHAPTER THREE

He spent the next couple of days going over the details regarding the stay at their old house near Lake Sonoma. He was able to secure the house for a week. That stretched their time by a few more days. He was hoping for a big family gathering while they were there. This gave him a couple of extra days to get a nice Friday dinner organized.

It was about an hour before his appointment with Lee. He checked in with himself. There was just one nightmare after the last one at the hotel. The same general feeling of shrouded darkness and light. In this dream he was in a clean, well-lit room. The light was coming from everywhere and nowhere at the same time. The room was surrounded by glass walls, and everywhere outside the room was pitch black. This time he was a teenager. He knew that the darkness was a threat to him. He stood next to one of the glass walls peering into that blackness. It was like a blanket had been thrown over the entire room. He was safe in the room, but outside was danger. As he stared into the pitch black, he saw a light move through it and toward him. The light grew into the shape of an angelic woman. She was dressed all in white. She came right up to where he was standing and touched the glass. It was as if she was saying that he would be okay, but she was also sad. He reached up in compassion to touch where she was, yet as he did, she started to fade away, back into the darkness. He didn't want her to leave. Yet she grew smaller till she was just a pinpoint of light and then disappeared. He felt safe while she was there, but now a feeling of dread overcame him.

As if on cue, he was suddenly up on top of the room, on the

roof, in the darkness, with a bunch of people touching him and laughing. He felt a strong need to get back into that well-lit room. He pushed his way around what looked like a porch all along the top of the room. There had to be a door back into the light somewhere. He moved through the laughing party people. He was beginning to panic. Suddenly he burst through the revelers into an open area of the porch. There was a door there but standing in front of it was a man all in black, pointing his finger at the teenage Mike.

There was something very fearful about this man. He slowly started stepping towards Mike. He tried to back up, but the man kept a slow, deliberate pace, his finger always pointing. Then Mike found himself stuck with his back against the railing. The man was nearly touching him. He backed further into the railing, and it broke. He went tumbling down into the oppressive darkness. He bounced like a steel plate across the ground. Then, like steel, he was frozen. He couldn't move. It was like someone was holding him down. He looked up and saw the same man from the roof now on the ground just above him; he was reaching down with his finger. He looked vaguely familiar, but he had a horrible, disfigured smile across his face. He was just about to touch Mike . . . Mike's own scream brought him out of that dream.

That was just last night. The return of these dreams concerned Mike the most. He had found a way to create a safe area within the nightmares when they did come. But now, the nightmares were suddenly overwhelming. And the man in the dream pointing, just like the man in white; though, for the man in white there were no feelings of fear. Mike had a feeling that he needed to talk with that man. Still, the man in the dream, pointing. Mike wondered if there was a connection.

One of the results of trauma was that the victims can become hyper-sensitive, hyper-vigilant. They have a heightened intuitive sense. He knew that a lot of the adults with ACEs would ignore their intuition. Partly because they didn't believe their own feelings and also because they didn't want to look weird in front of their peers just because they were being themselves, following their own inner thoughts.

The birthright of the abused child was to spend much of their lives hiding from themselves, hiding themselves from others. Something Mike thought he had left in a darker past, not trusting his inner self. Mike had learned to trust his instincts. Though sometimes, even in his day-to-day activities, he sometimes felt like he was living in an otherworldly experience, for lack of a better description. Like he was walking beside himself and checking in on every move or conversation he was engaging.

Then, other times, he felt like he was tuned in to some inexplicable psychic experience. For example, when his brother took his life, Mike was on the opposite side of the continent. It was late at night, and he was sipping on a glass of wine when he heard a loud bang and then a thud of something falling on his back porch.

"Kevin just shot himself." He said with complete confidence to his wife. In his mind he thought, *it wasn't unexpected. Still-*

"What?"

"Kevin just shot himself," he said again. She looked at him, shook her head and went back to reading. Three hours later they received the phone call from Mike's deeply grieving mother. Kevin had killed himself. His wife, Virginia, looked at him like he was from another world.

This type of thing has happened a couple of times. Mike was thinking about the strangeness of knowing for certain that something bad was about to happen. Like he was having some sort of prescient feeling, just before the experience. He puzzled over those few incidents that he had had in the past. Another was when a woman was coming down some stairs and he knew she was going to fall, she did. In his logical mind he thought, *is it because of some hyperconscious feeling expressing itself, an intuitive vignette, a spark of heightened awareness beyond the understanding of our present science; a spiritual mystery?* Then he thought, *though often, many of those things in the past, that we humans have called a mystery or spiritual were later explained by science. I don't know.* The last thought made him feel a little better. He believed in science.

Perhaps it was some type of heightened intuitive sense. Like when we can feel someone is looking at us, or that oppressive silence. Like when you're on a hike and suddenly it's silent and there's a gnawing feeling that something dangerous is lurking. Or maybe it was just dumb empirical luck. Still, something was churning at his gut. In last night's dream it was the disfigured man in a hooded black outfit pointing at him, and now the man in white. *Is there a connection? Why now?*

A question he would have for Lee. He had not seen that man in white since their first encounter. Still, it felt like they were connected. It was like he needed to tell Mike something, but then he disappeared. Mike felt like his life was suddenly a chapter in some magical realism story. Except it didn't feel magical. Lee's office was at the far end of the Art District, so he had decided to walk to his appointment.

The meeting with Lee was a good one. Because of their history as close friends, Mike trusted her and her therapeutic expertise. They talked about the feeling of terror that had returned to his dreams. She reminded him that he had achieved the ability to become an adult, protecting the child, in his nightmares. She suggested that he practice feeling like the adult in his mind during the day. She asked if he had previously worked or practiced with EMDR. He told her that he had experienced Eye Movement Desensitization and Reprocessing before with much success. She seemed pleased and referred him to another therapist for a professional session. He understood. They were very close friends, and she was concerned about her independence if she were the one to analyze and try to help him; and of course she was a professional.

She gave him the phone number to a local psychologist, Dr. Suzanne Lowell, PsyD. In the meantime, she reminded him of the importance of his network of supportive friends and family. He told her about the family gathering and then invited her to join them for the dinner he was planning. Even though this wasn't an analysis, being a professional, she told him to ask her after he had set up his treatment with Dr. Lowell. As soon as he left, he called and set that appointment. Then he called Lee, told her he had talked with the therapist and asked her again to join the family for dinner.

"Well, that was quick," she said with a small laugh. "Let me think about it. It would be nice to see your girls again: It's been a few years. We'll talk, I'm sure." He finished talking with Lee and popped the phone back into its holder, strapped to his waist. He knew, with confidence, that they would connect.

As he walked, he noticed that the Art District was busy. It was getting late in the afternoon. Some of the shops would be closing soon. Then he thought about the weekend. That made him smile.

There was always work that could be done when you're a writer. Planning, writing or, most importantly, research, but he didn't feel like working. So, he decided to do a whole lot of nothing over the weekend. He did have a meeting with his two girls on Wednesday. They were to meet the ranch caretaker around 4 o'clock and finalize their responsibilities and agreements for staying at the house. In the meantime, he would do some planning but also watch some baseball and maybe binge something on Netflix.

"Are you Michael Smith?" A woman's voice brought him out of his head.

"Yes, I am." He looked toward the voice and there was a young woman, maybe in her mid-thirties.

"I read your book on a healing heart; healing from abuse I mean. It was the right message at the right time. Thank you." She held out her hand.

"I'm glad it helped you. How are you doing?" He shook her hand.

"I'm okay. Mostly good days. Do you think we could talk for a moment?" It looked to Mike like she needed to talk. He could never say no. One of the effects he had come to experience from his ACEs; he had a need to save the world.

"Sure. We could get a beverage at Sisters."

"I'd be grateful." She seemed relieved.

They were about a block and a half from the restaurant. Mike gestured and they walked together in silence for a minute or two.

"What's your name?" Mike broke the silence.

"Elizabeth." Mike stopped and looked at her. This had to be a crazy coincidence. Still, the timing and the name shook him for a second.

"Are you all right?" She looked concerned, like she did something wrong.

"Yes, sorry, I just . . . sorry. I'm fine, shall we?" He gestured toward the restaurant. He regained most of his composure. She nodded and moved in step with him.

"Did I say something that bothered you? If so, I'm really sorry. We don't have to meet if you don't want to."

"No, it's just that you inadvertently reminded me of something that recently happened. It wasn't good. I'll leave it at that."

"I'm really sorry."

"It's not your fault."

"Still . . . sorry."

"You say sorry a lot."

"I've been told that." As she said that she thought of something. Whatever she was remembering made her sad.

They made their way into Sisters, got their preferred beverages and came back out and sat at one of the sidewalk tables in front of the restaurant. After a couple of sips Elizabeth broke the silence.

"Do you have occasions where you still experience any of the long-term negative effects from your childhood abuse?"

Mike looked at her. Her timing was incredible, or maybe just coincidental. Her name, Elizabeth, and the timing of her question again made him shut down for a few seconds.

"Did I do it again?" She said as she watched his puzzled look. He thought about saying, "No" but opted for honesty.

"Yes."

"I'm so sorry. Maybe this isn't a good idea." She started to rise.

"Don't be sorry. Please, sit. I am fully responsible for my emotional self. Yes. First you unintentionally reminded me of a young mom I met earlier, whose name was Elizabeth, who took her own life sometime after a brief meeting with me. Secondly, I just came from an advice session with my therapist friend because I am experiencing some past trauma, some toxic stress. So, to your question, yes, I am having a period of regression. I am reliving some of the painful moments of my past, including my brother's suicide."

"Oh my gosh, I read about that in your book. I'm truly, truly sorry."

"You do say sorry a lot."

"I'm s–" She put her hand over her lips and smiled at knowing she was just about to say it again.

"I get it. It's a reaction to and from our abuse. It's almost as if we are saying, 'I'm sorry I'm here, it's my fault.' Of course it is not, and it never was. That's why it's important for us to find self-compassion, the love of self, and forgive ourselves for all the guilt and shame that never should have been ours to bear." Elizabeth nodded her head.

"How can I help you?" Mike added.

"I just broke up with Jeremy, an abusive man, my second in a row. Not physically abusive . . ." She went into her memory for a second, "Like Jim. No, Jeremy was verbally abusive. I don't know which is worse. He would use his male voice to control me in many ways. Just like when I was a young teen, the powerful voice of authority. The voice of my father. When I'm confronted with someone, someone that yells at me in anger, especially a man, I freeze. I just panic and shut down. Right now, if there's any duress, even just deciding over what I would like in a cup of coffee, if I feel pressured, I feel panic starting to build in my gut and I shut down or I run from the situation till I feel safe. Through therapy I was getting better, but lately–"

"Are you not in therapy?"

"My recent therapist is a man. I can't seem to open to him. He's kind, he asks good questions, at least that I can tell, but I can't seem to drop my guard with him."

"Just like you being in control of your life experience, you are in control of who helps you. Your therapist will not take it personally if you tell him that you would rather work with a woman. He's a professional. He knows his job is to help you, even if it means recommending you to another therapist."

"Yes, I do know." She seemed very sad at that moment.

"I'm concerned. You do know about the 988 Hotline?"

"Yes."

"If you're struggling and can't reach your counselor, please use it. They've helped a lot of people."

"I will, I promise."

"I believe you."

"Well, I should let you get on with your day. Thank you for taking the time to talk with me and to listen."

"Any time, and that's not a throw away, I mean any time. Also don't hesitate to say hi if you see me on the street again."

"I hope someday to achieve the same level of compassion, confidence and forgiveness that you seem to have."

"Well, I have twenty plus years or more of experience than you. In society it takes time till your expectations become reality, and for us, the abused ones, it takes longer. Keep talking, keep questioning and with professional help, keep healing."

"I will. By the way I am sor – Oops, I almost said it again." They both smiled, "what I mean is I feel for your loss. I'm sure your brother, wherever he may be, is proud of you." Emotions took over Mike and he had to clench his teeth to keep from tearing up.

"Thank you. It appears that I have too much empathy."

"If you ask me, this world could use a lot more empathy." She said that with much conviction.

"I think you're going to be just fine." Mike said. She smiled and started to leave.

"Oh, one more thing. You have left that abusive man behind. And as a suggestion, purely based on my personal experience, don't let yourself fall into another relationship for a few or more years at least. I took eight years. We wounded children, still trying to grow up as adults, often get into a partnership because we feel like that's what we're supposed to do. But, because we're still fearful of being ourselves, we just try to please, to become what we think the other partner expects, as opposed to just growing together in a healthy relationship. We become chameleons and try to camouflage our insecurities by acting in a way we think will please our partner.

"Go out on dates. Have fun with your girlfriends and guy friends. If you can, try to get a place by yourself or with a girlfriend. I promise you that during the time you take to be on your own you will learn a lot about yourself. Maybe even learn to like who you are. Just a suggestion. Talk with your new therapist, I think she'll agree."

"Well, till I find a roommate I am by myself as I kicked Jeremy out."

"Don't let him worm his way back into your life."

"Oh, that's not going to happen. He's been warned. And, just so you know, I am beginning to like me." She said confidently.

"Good! Also, try not to consume too much alcohol alone. Again, based on my own experience, these are thoughts for you to consider, talk with your therapist, please."

"Yeah, I will. Also, I am no longer a drinker. That was my father, just the smell of it would remind me of him while he was above me. No, that's not an issue." Her hatred for her father was evident on her face. "Thank you again for your time. Have a good day." She smiled at Mike, then turned and walked back toward the Art District.

Mike watched her leave. She was a wounded soul, but he had a good feeling about her. He picked up the cups from the table and dropped them into the bus tray just inside the restaurant door. It was just around 6 pm on this late spring day. He started walking up A St. As he was getting closer to where he took the alleyway toward his house, his phone buzzed. It was his sister in Kentucky. A couple of years ago their mother had died. Every now and then his sister, Lana, would send a text remembering their mom. This time she sent, "Mom really loved this time of the year." Mike texted back, "Yeah, she did." That was it. It was usually a short communication. They both reacted differently to their mother. As far as Mike was concerned his mom bore some responsibility for the abuse her kids went through. His other sister, Arlene, had barely talked to their mom. She wanted retribution. She fully blamed their mom for letting the abuse happen.

Just a year or so before she passed Lana confronted their mom and asked if she knew what was happening to her children. She said she did and offered an apology. Lana stopped her and said she didn't want to know anything more. She had this image of her mom she didn't want to let go. Mike didn't blame her. Lana was the youngest and managed to avoid the terrible abuse from their stepdad. Years later she confessed to Mike, "At night I used to put a chair up against the door handle of my room. I knew something bad was going on, but I didn't experience it. Like all the kids in our family, I left as soon as I could."

All this pulled his brother, Kevin, back to the front of his mind. Then he thought, *hopefully this rough time isn't going to last long. I miss you, brother. I do all this work, these seminars, all this healing in memory of you. I'm sorry I wasn't there to try to talk you out of suicide. I don't know what I could have done, but I would have tried. I wish I could've seen you one more time.* Home was now in view.

"Tonight will be a good night to binge-watch something," he said to himself as he got closer.

CHAPTER FOUR

"Hola, Mr. Smith, I know you are familiar with the system, still I need to go over it with you." They were standing in front of the garage. The caretaker gestured toward the hills at the back of the property. That's where most of the irrigation water came from. A perennial stream flowed from the hills behind the property down into a pond used by the house and a winery next door. Mike had set up a couple of small reservoirs up in the hills and from them ran the water through various hoses about three hundred yards down into a tank. The tank was high enough to gravity feed water to the yard and garden.

Rose had her newborn strapped to her front. She and her sister Sarah along with Tyler and the four-year-old were exploring the main house while Zeus was running and sniffing around the backyard, no doubt remembering the property. They say animals don't have a sense of time. Perhaps he thought they all just went on a trip and now they're back at home. He was a good dog.

"Yes, I remember," Mike responded to the caretaker, Alonzo.

"So, as you probably recall, the lines get air bubbles in them and every now and then you need to release that pressure so the water can flow."

"Got it."

"Okay, I will set some firewood for you on the front porch. If you should need more, it's by the fence in the backyard. I'll leave my contact information along with the short-term rental agreement on the desk in the foyer. There is a charging plug for an electric car, in the garage, in case anybody needs it." Alonzo started walking toward the front entrance as he spoke.

"Thank you, Alonzo. We're looking forward to staying here."

"Oh, since you and the owners know each other and even though your short-term guest agreement doesn't start till next Wednesday, a week from today, they told me to let you know you can start bringing things to the house on Monday, if you want. The current lock code to the front door is on the paperwork, also on the desk. There are no other guests in contract till after your visit. So, they asked me to tell you to 'please make yourself at home'."

"Thank you again. How are the trails along the creek and into the hills? Still in good shape?"

"Yes. One of the owners is a bit fragile, so I keep the trails clean and brush free."

"Great. My girls spent a lot of time in those hills."

"It is beautiful. Do know that a mountain lion has been spotted roaming around these properties lately. Also, don't forget about the ticks, they're extra bad this year."

"Yeah, I remember those nasty arachnids. I'll ask the kids to stay together and carry a pitchfork or something when they go walking in the hills. Just as a precaution to the puma. Thank you again."

"Yes, sir. I've a few things to do so you guys can revisit the house and property for about another half hour. Then I need to lock up."

"Fair enough. I'll go talk with the kids. Thanks again, Alonzo." The caretaker nodded and walked off toward the utility shed. Mike walked into the foyer. The new owners had put an upright piano in the foyer across from the desk. He ran his hand over the keys just to hear a crescendo. He walked over to the desk and took a minute to verify the paperwork and front door code.

"Dad! Come, check it out, they put a game room in the upstairs area where we used to play hide and seek." Sarah was clearly excited. Upstairs originally had a kid's bedroom with a small porch and TV room. Because of the deep angle of the roof much of the upstairs area was storage. There was one spot where another small bedroom was created after Rose was born. They called it the hobbit room because adults had to duck to get through the door as well as in certain areas of the room. Otherwise, the upstairs was mostly open. There was one spot next to Sarah's old room where the new owners created a small playroom with an air hockey table, a small bar and TV. It was well done. Mike made his way up to that playroom.

"Wow, this is really nice." Mike said as he watched Rose and Tyler's four-year-old try to slide the pucks across the air hockey table. She was having as much fun as the adults.

"Did you see, Dad? The lines you and mom marked to measure our growth are still on the door frame in the kitchen." Rose had a big smile.

"Yeah, you can still see the tiny number 15 next to my last measurement line. Thank you, Dad, for this one last time at our old house. Hey, do you want to play a game of table hockey?" It was Sarah.

"No, sorry, we have to leave in the next twenty minutes or so. Alonzo has to lock down the house. I promise while we are here, I will kick your butt on table hockey."

"Ha! In your dreams. I've been practicing."

"Oh, I guess I'm in trouble." Mike smiled.

"Uh huh, bring it on!" She laughed. Her laugh was contagious. Everybody laughed. "Challenge laid down and accepted!" Sarah announced to everyone in the room. Truth be told, Tyler would probably beat anybody there. Well, except for Walker, the four-year-old. For some reason she always seemed to beat her dad in competitive sports. Tyler was a good dad.

"We should get Zeus and make our way out of here. Oh, Alonzo said we can start settling in on Monday. He means like stocking the fridge and such," Mike said to the crew. "So, let's head out for today. We'll shop in Healdsburg over the weekend." Suddenly everybody was drawn to a peculiar sound. With which Mike was familiar. It was an old sound in his memory. It went, thump-thump, giggle-giggle . . . thump-thump, giggle-giggle. Mike smiled.

"Where's Walker?" Rose asked. They all followed the sound

and there was Walker sliding down the stairs on her butt, giggling to herself. Everybody started to laugh, which, of course, got Walker to laugh louder and make bigger thumps down the stairs. Like all small children she enjoyed being the center of attention. She slid down to the bottom and turned to them all. "Your turn Daddy, your turn."

"Okay little one, here I come." Tyler slid down to Walker, quickly followed by Sarah. Rose chose to walk down the stairs since she had her infant swaddled to her torso.

"Grandpa Mike, your turn," Walker shouted at Mike.

"That's okay, sweetheart. My sliding on my butt days are over. But it sure was fun to watch you."

"Okay." Walker climbed up a few stairs and with much glee slid down again. Both Rose and Sarah did the same thing when they were little. Mike tried to hold back the emotional sweetness of that memory. The kids saw it on his face.

"Oh, there goes Dad," Sarah said. Rose looked up and laughed. "We love you, Dad."

"I love you all back." That was it. The happy tears filled his eyes, followed by some sniffling. "Okay, okay, we should make our way out of here. Alonzo will be taking off soon and he wants to lock up the house."

"C'mon Walker, let's go find Zeus." Rose, Walker and baby went to get their dog.

"Hey, Mike, you're springing for most of this get-away, how about Rose and I take you out for dinner?" It was Tyler.

"And me . . ." It was Sarah.

"And, of course, you." Tyler laughed as he responded to Sarah. She smiled.

"What do you say?" Tyler asked.

"That sounds really good," Mike said.

"Okay, cool, we're on. There's a nice sushi restaurant in Healdsburg. In about an hour?" Mike nodded. "Great! I'll let Rose know and we'll see you there." With that he left.

"He's a good man," Mike said to Sarah as they walked toward the front of the house.

"Yes, he is. You know Dad, we've had our issues, but I think you're a good man too."

"Thanks, daughter. I sometimes cringe over the past. Wishing I could have been wiser or better or done things different–"

"How human of you, Dad. Everything that has happened before this moment makes us who we are now and who we will be. Whatever the past, I think you turned out okay."

"You always were the wise one. Your sister, the practical one, but you, you can see and understand things better than, well, anyone I know."

"I know."

"And your confidence in yourself." Mike smiled as he said that; so did Sarah.

"Mr. Mike, I'm done for today. Are you all about ready?"

"Yes, Alonzo, we're done. I would like to start loading some groceries into the house this weekend, if that's okay?"

"My wife and I were going to use this weekend to clean and get the house ready. If you need to, that's fine, but try to aim for Sunday afternoon. If you don't mind?"

"Not at all and thank you."

"Oh, don't forget the gate code." Alonzo reminded Mike.

"Right. Thank you. I'll take the paperwork now." Mike gathered the house information and exited along with Sarah. Alonzo locked up the house.

"Okay, Mr. Mike, enjoy your stay and if you need help with anything about the house, just call."

"We will Alonzo, thank you."

Alonzo nodded and turned towards his truck near the utility shed. Tyler and gang were just finishing loading up their Tahoe.

"See you both at the restaurant in about forty?" Tyler said.

"We'll be there."

"Yes, we will," Sarah shouted. She gave Mike a hug and got into her car. Alonzo had already left. Tyler was the first of the family to leave, followed by Sarah. Mike was by himself. He looked at the house and the property. Though he and his wife separated while they were still living here, there were some good memories tied to the house and land. It took a lot of hard work and yes, luck, to have the young family move from the East Bay to just north of Lake Sonoma. Sarah was around four years old when they were finally able to move here. It needed some work. Eventually they fixed it up and lived there for years, till life got in the way. He regretted the negative changes that they endured as the family split apart but was deeply grateful that they all managed to find a way to still be together.

His wife had remarried to a real good man. Mike had chosen not to remarry. Eventually Tyler, Rose, her mom and her new husband, Bill, moved to the coast, about two hours away from Santa Rosa. Recently, and because he worked as a writer, he was thinking about joining them. *If I could just find a place that's affordable.* He thought to himself. He took one more look around.

"This will be good." He said to himself with a smile. He made his way to his car. He hadn't spent much time in Healdsburg since the family had separated years ago. He had some time, so he decided he would go and explore the town before dinner with the kids. With one last look he drove up the dirt driveway and out to Dutcher Creek Rd.

CHAPTER FIVE

"Okay Mike, so far, good. You have experienced EMDR before. Your previous adaptive information and processing is remarkable in that you mostly did it yourself. You have been able to transform a devastating childhood nightmare into something somewhat more positive by becoming the adult in these difficult dreams." Mike sat in a comfortable chair across from Dr. Suzanne Lowell PsyD.

"Yes. A good therapist I was working with, gosh, twenty years ago asked me, 'Why don't you find a way in your dreams to be the adult protecting the abused and fearful child in your nightmares.' So, I did, and she was spot on."

"I see. The serendipitous discovery of EMDR was made by the psychologist, Francine Shapiro, because of her own experience with her eye movement."

"I do know that now, but not when I figured out how to be the adult in my nightmares."

"I get it. You have a strong sense of self. You were determined not to let the abuse that happened to you as a child control your adult life. It's during certain dreams that our eyes go into REM, and it probably was during that rapid eye movement you were able to successfully bring the adult Mike into your nightmare and protect that abused and fearful child. Doing this by yourself is truly impressive, but now you say that the abusive dreams are returning but without the adult helping the child. Is that right?"

"Yes."

"Okay, I feel confident that we can start work within the intermediate phases of an EMDR therapy as long as you do."

"I trust your expertise, Dr. Lowell. Just tell me what I need to do to help you help me."

"Great. I work with music to help the bilateral tactile movement, your eye movement. You have chosen one of Beethoven's Sonatas to establish a rhythm you feel comfortable with. I am now putting that on, but at a low volume. You, as I instruct, are to close your eyes while you move them, like REM, to the right and left within the rhythm of Sonata 14 Opus 27. Also, if you should feel it, gently tap your fingers on your legs along with the rhythm. Okay. I do have some questions I would like to ask before we engage in EMDR." Dr. Lowell said as she turned the player on at a very low frequency.

"Cool, ask away."

"You can close your eyes while we talk."

"Okay."

"Looking back, in what ways did your mother express her love for you?"

"Her closeness. I could feel her affection when she was holding me."

"Okay, and you loved your mother?"

"Yes, but . . ."

"But?"

"That's one part of my confusion and conflict."

"Can you tell me more about the confusion or conflict, or both?"

"It was like she disappeared when us kids needed her the most. She loved us, that feels right, but why she wasn't there to save us from her mother . . . and from her second husband, confuses and makes me angry."

"You say she wasn't there, where do you think she was?"

"I don't know. In those terrible moments of abuse, I was trying to just get by, to survive. She should have been there to help us." Mike's last statement was bitter.

"At the risk of passing judgement, would you say she let you down?"

"In that aspect, yes. All of us."

"Okay, what about your biological father, what did you love about him?"

"When I was a kid, nine-ish, both Kevin and I thought he was cool. I mean, he made monster movies and bought us kid stuff, so we thought he was really cool."

"Hmm, and do you think that's how he showed you his love?"

"Well, I thought as much when I was nine, but I saw who he really was before I reached ten. He was a con man. He was nice looking, and he talked a good line of bullshit. That was part of his ability to enmesh those who were close to him, to pull people into his fantasy world and then manipulate them. He was a fraud. There were people he had convinced in Hollywood that he was a great movie producer. Apparently quite easy to do back in the late fifties and into the sixties. He persuaded people to give him money, which he never intended to repay and then used that same con power to pretend to be some great Hollywood player making great movies with their money. Which he wasn't. As long as you supported him and his ideas, he made you feel like you were the greatest."

"Did he make you feel like you were the greatest?"

"Yes, sometimes, but I soon learned he only cared about how other people perceived him. I remember a designer that had worked for him on the monster movie he was making at the time. There are pictures of me and Kevin riding down Hollywood Blvd. in the open area of a pick-up truck with the sponge rubber monster next to us, because he wanted everyone to see his latest creation. He only really cared about his image, not us, not even the movie he was trying to make. I believe he called it the 'Creeping Terror.' Which, every now and then, appeared on Mystery Science Theater 3000.

"Anyway, the designer wanted to be paid for his work, building the monster. My father refused for reasons that I do not know, but the designer left our house in such anger that he completely splintered the front screen door. My father just laughed. He also played women all the time. Whenever my brother Kevin and I went to visit him, he made us feel like he was the greatest Dad in the world. Still, we had to deal with his numerous girlfriends.

"But when he didn't get what he wanted, he hurt people, sometimes physically. I remember one night when my brother and I were in bed when this crazy drunk man came to visit our little cement house, just off Hollywood Boulevard, and the girl that was our babysitter that night was in the front room. She was beaten so badly that as we lay in bed, in fear, we heard her cries go from help to tears to just moans. That is what I mostly remember of my father. My brother, sadly, eventually, when I don't know, chose to be like our father. Maybe it wasn't a choice, maybe it was his fate? I don't know."

"You said you were in your bed, do you know for sure it was your father that hurt the babysitter?"

"Yes, Kevin and I peeked through the hallway door to see who it was. It was horrible."

"What do you feel about him now?"

"My brother?"

"That's another discussion. No, your father?"

"I hate him."

"That was a quick response." Mike could hear her writing.

"It's the weird thing that keeps me from hating my mother. I now see that she had this need to stay with or even this need to have some value in a man's eyes. She loved us, that I know to be true, but she failed badly to protect us. She was probably told to mind her own business. Which, sadly, she did. We should have been her business. She just did what her man told her to do, perhaps out of fear.

"When I was little, I remember her being thrown across the kitchen floor, blood crisscrossed on the linoleum by her knees as she crawled and cried big tears, and my father with intense anger and hate running after her. I hate him. He hurt people.

"You tell me that it was fortunate that I was able to help myself through my dreams. I have always had an adaptive brain. Perhaps it was a necessity. Perhaps a bit of genetic luck, still I can pull memories from all the way back to when I was two. The nightmares of his abusive treatment against my mother haunt me. In those dreams I'm always the small child where things are moving too fast and out of my control, and all I can do is scream, 'stop'! I know those nightmares to be related to the misogynistic abuse by my blood father. But the nightmares about my physical/sexual abuse are from childhood episodes that my brain, and rightfully so, has disassociated. The abusive adult faces are blurred and the dark blanket, or whatever, being pulled over my head, the complete helplessness of being held down while I scream; those are the nightmares that cause me to wake up in a sweat and cry in a little boy's voice. Those are the horrific dreams that have returned."

"Okay, you clearly have been in therapy before; you've written very helpful books. You've done your research, yet now, Mike, something is creating or, perhaps exacerbating, an internal conflict. Let's see what we can do to help that little boy. Before we start, is there anything you could identify as an emotional or physical trigger that may have happened to you recently?"

"I don't know. The seminars have been rough lately. Oh, yes, at the last seminar a woman approached at the end. She was clearly depressed and wanted to talk. As we did, I could see that she was not in a good place. I reminded her of the suicide hotline, 988, and encouraged her to seek professional help. She said she was looking for a new therapist, and she was familiar with the hotline. She was going through a rough time with a separation from her abusive husband and his control over their children. Just before our conversation ended, I told her, 'Do the right thing', meaning for her kids. She left behind a note and in it she said, 'Tell Mr. Smith I think I did the right thing'." Mike stopped there and tears started to fill his eyes. He opened his eyes to wipe them and to dry up some sniffles.

"I'm so sorry Mike. You know it's not your fault."

"Intellectually, yes. Still, for some reason, it pulled the past right up into my face."

"All right, let's take a minute." Dr. Lowell wrote a few more things on her pad. "Mike, your little boy nightmares seem to follow a general pattern of darkness, restraint and fear. If you were to single out a specific dream, which one and why?"

"Well, there is one I had as a young boy that never repeated. It was mysterious and, to this day, I don't know if it was real or not. I've never forgotten it."

"In what way, mysterious?"

"We, meaning Kevin and myself, were at our grandmother's house. The adults were having a party. They were laughing and whooping it up and talking over each other. Kevin and I were in the other room, and my mom came in and demanded we go to bed. A bed on the floor of a room upstairs had been set aside for us. There was already a big bed in the room, yet we were on a small mattress on the floor beside the bed. Anyway, we were ordered, 'go to bed'.

"As littles we learned not to argue with our partying adults. One of my stepfather's famous laugh lines was, 'Kids should be seen and not heard.' So, we obeyed. We made our way to the stairs and turned on the light. I started climbing the stairs and looked up and at the top there was this person dressed as a clown. She looked a lot like my grandmother. Yet, she had this look of such sadness, infinite sadness, as she looked back down at me. I froze in fear. I knew my grandmother was in the other room with all the adults. Kevin was standing right behind me looking the same as I was feeling.

"I started yelling for my mother. I told her there was somebody standing at the top of the stairs. She angrily told us to stop fooling around and get to bed. The clown was still there so we yelled for our mom again, "There's someone at the top of the stairs!" We were clearly scared. She, angry that we were disturbing her, hurried over and looked up the stairs. And, of course, no one was there. I pleaded with her that there was some sad-looking woman dressed like a clown at the top of the stairs. With an angry look of disbelief she slapped me hard and yelled at me to 'get to bed'. Kevin quickly moved up the stairs." Mike stopped, clearly remembering that moment.

"What did you feel after your mom slapped you?" Dr. Lowell interjected.

"I remember it hurt to tears, but I also remember thinking, why? I scurried up the stairs after Kevin for fear of more punishment."

"Understandably so."

"We crawled onto our mattress on the floor. We were quiet for a moment and then I asked Kevin, 'you did see that bitter sad-looking clown, right?' He convinced me that he did, but I learned later in life that Kevin would tell me whatever I wanted to hear.

"Then the attic door at the foot of the bed started to slowly open. Not like it was because of a breeze. No. It looked as if it were creeping open. Kevin and I, already distraught, started screaming. This time my stepfather came up the stairs, stood outside the door with a belt in his hands. 'If I come in there, I'm going to use this.' He showed us a belt, and we stifled our noise into a whimper. 'That's what I thought,' he said as he headed back down the stairs.

"After he was gone the attic door started to open again. Kevin couldn't help it and screamed. At that our stepfather yelled, 'Do I need to come in there,' from the bottom of the stairs. We both yelled 'No!' The door continued to quietly open. I pushed and then followed Kevin underneath the big bed. We held each other and then I felt someone touch my foot. And that's the last thing I remember of that dream."

"That dream seems very detailed."

"All my dreams are deeply detailed."

"What I'm wondering is do you think it was a dream, or do you think it was real?"

"That's why I'm bringing it up. You asked what dream I would remember. All my life I have wondered the same thing, was it real or a dream? I honestly don't know. Still, I have never forgotten it."

"Okay, let's talk about that, and see if we can help that little boy. Listen to the rhythm of the music, Mike, and shortly we'll start." To give Mike a moment, she slightly adjusted the music's volume. It was one of several choices the doctor gave her patients. It would last as long as she needed. She sat her notebook on her lap and clicked her pen a couple of times. "All right, Mike, sit back and close your eyes. Find the music and let it guide your eye movement. Every now and then I am going to check-in. Okay?"

"Yes. Let's go."

"Okay, relax."

The session was good. Mike had set another appointment and left after her summary. It was late in the afternoon as he walked back towards his house. He was just about to South A St. when his phone rang. It was his daughter Sarah.

"Hello, sweetheart. What's up?"

"Hi, Dad. I'm here in Santa Rosa, and I thought I'd check in and see if you wanted to get together?"

"Great, where are you?"

"I'm just at the edge of the Art District."

"Perfect timing. I'm just getting to South A St. How about we get a cup of tea or something and catch up?"

"Sounds good. Meet at Sisters?"

"Nice, I'll see you shortly."

"Okay, on my way."

The thought of seeing his daughter lifted his mood even more. He was near the corner of South A St. and Sebastopol Ave. He picked up his pace a bit as he wanted an outdoor seat at the restaurant.

It was a late spring afternoon, and the weather was nearly perfect. This was the time of year when it began to warm up in Sonoma County, but today it was sunny and moderate. Mike had purchased a cup of tea and grabbed a sidewalk table in front of Sisters. He just had a sip when Sarah walked into view from Sebastopol Ave. He waved as she saw him. She made her way to his table.

"Hi, Dad," She said, setting some shopping bags next to the table. "I'm just going to get a cup of tea." She said as she gave him a quick hug.

"Can I get you an early dinner?"

"No, thanks Dad. I just want some tea. Be right back." As she left Mike's phone chimed. It was Lee. That made Mike smile.

He just came out of an excellent session with Dr. Lowell, so he was already in good spirits. It struck Mike how, following a successful therapeutic session, colors seemed more vibrant, and his feet seemed lighter on the ground. Then having his number one daughter reach out to him and then Lee, he was smiling.

"Hey there, I just finished my session with Dr. Lowell."

"I was guessing about the timing. How did it go?"

"She was the right recommendation. Thank you. It went well. So, am I going to see you next Friday?"

"That's why I am calling. I would love to join you for a family dinner."

"Well, that makes me very happy. I look forward to it. It's been a while, but you know the address, right?"

"I remember. I'm looking forward to it. I have a client coming soon, so, bye for now, but we'll connect soon and thank you. I'm glad you had a good session, Mike. See you soon."

"Yeah, same, looking forward to seeing you. Bye for now." Mike ended the call as Sarah walked out of Sister's.

"So, Dad, how are you?" she asked when she sat down.

"I'm well. Just had a session with Dr. Lowell. I always feel better after a session. She's a good one. And you? How are you?"

"I'm really good, thanks. Very much looking forward to our time together at the ranch."

"Same. It'll be nice to catch up. I don't get to see you as often as I would like, now that you live in The City."

"I know. This will be a fun family gathering. I especially like your idea of the big dinner on Friday. So, who's Dr. Lowell?" It was someone new to her.

"Yes. She was recommended by Lee, whom I just got off the phone with. Oh, by the way, I invited Lee to our family dinner. I hope that's okay?"

"Of course it is. I always liked her. So, anything new in seminars or writing?"

"The seminars have been rough lately. One of the things we talked about in therapy. Writing, that's a different story. I'm trying to get a better understanding of what a female goes through with her experience regarding abuse. I want to write about it. It's a sad fact that young girls are much more likely to be abused than their male counterparts. Not to take anything away from the young boys that are abused. That's my latest research project." Sarah looked at him for a good twenty seconds.

"Hmm, first of all, Dad, you, as a man, cannot entirely empathize with a female experience. You have a great deal of empathy in your heart, but to empathize with being female, you cannot. Secondly, and outside of childhood rape and abuse, which is terrible on its own, girls go through various forms of abuse throughout their life. Sadly, it happens in all cultures. Primarily because of the way men perceive their relationship to girls. When men can start to think beyond their sex organs or their physical dominance, it will be a different world."

"What do you mean, I can't have empathy?"

"Well, any person that feels like they can rape or abuse a child should be shot."

"No argument there." Mike went into his mind. He was conflicted. *Or kill themselves.* Mike thought about his brother. He has learned, through his sister, that Kevin had improperly touched his niece, though Mike wanted to believe he had never raped or physically attacked anyone. Yet, what he did to his niece was wrong. Kevin wasn't a big man, just a real good conman, like his blood father. Still, Mike remembered how close they were as kids. To this day he believed Kevin would still be alive if it weren't for the terrible abuse they went through as kids. He knew his brother had crossed the line in perpetuating that abuse. Still, the memories of their time together. He loved his brother.

Sarah continued, "Yeah, anyway, outside that horrible experience of childhood rape and abuse, girls go through various stages of male creepiness and unwanted attention or touching. Dar Williams wrote a beautiful song titled, 'When I was a Boy.' In the song she wistfully talks about her young days, before she started that long and often confusing road to womanhood. She remembered that she could wrestle and run and sling a sword like Peter Pan as good as any boy. Then the change.

"That happens to every little girl. There is not a society on this planet that honors or educates preteens about that. Sure, there are religious ceremonies' like Bar and Bat Mitzvahs, and others, yet none recognize the dangers and confusion of suddenly being viewed as a sexual being. Probably because almost all our societies are patriarchal. You can't understand how it feels when suddenly one day all the boys start staring at your chest. How they start telling you how pretty you are, even though you didn't ask. How they suddenly want to put their hands on you, not because we're playing football or rugby or any other physical sport. No, they want to touch you because they are driven by their immature prurient mind or to own you, or even worse, they just feel entitled.

"Sure, there's a certain amount of innocence. You suddenly go from being a happy child to being looked at with different levels of desire. Sure, some of it is male stupidity and inability to understand what's proper or not, but then some of it is nothing short of leering and creepiness, if that's such a word. All young girls go through that."

"I'm sorry, honey. I was a slow one to that male desire, but it happened. I remember playing football with a young female friend. I mean she was tough. One day I tackled her and accidentally grabbed her chest. I was mortified and apologized. She kind of just blew it off. It was no big deal. But our relationship changed after that. I remember stopping by her house one day and shouting for her to come out and play. We were around twelve years old. Instead of her coming to the door she popped up in her bathroom window, clearly topless, though not exposed and chatted with me for about twenty minutes.

"The point being she was flirting. And even in my young boy's mind I kinda knew that, and I remember I thought 'wow she's pretty'. It was something that had not even entered my mind, prior to her flirting with me. I mean that was more innocent than anything else. Still, I remember that first experience I had at how I looked at my female friends. It was like somebody had flipped a switch and all the girls looked different."

"Well, that flipped switch is different for girls. Part of that switch is the skin-crawling experience of a male's unwanted desire, attention, and the rude comments at a young girl's sudden, to men, process of physically turning into a woman. Not the innocent flirting or youthful silliness and mistakes that the young make, it was that a lot of men, grown men, were leering and trying to touch or even kiss me when I was just trying to be a twelve-year-old kid."

"Where? Who tried to mess with you. I will beat the shit out of 'em."

"Dad, calm down. There's nothing you can do now. Let me finish. Outside of the sick men, of which there are plenty, that inevitable shift from the girl that played Peter Pan, as in Dar's song, to early womanhood is short of a creepy experience that a young girl has to face.

"Then you get into my age. Those same creepy men are still there. Now I know and can see them, sadly. But now, I, we must watch our backs. I mean when I go into a parking lot, especially if it's late, I carry my keys in between my fingers, with one key pointed out like a knife, in case I have to defend myself.

"It's sad that half of the human population has to be careful of where they are just because of the other half. We like to think of ourselves as civilized, but I tell you what, Dad, the day a woman can walk down any dark street and not fear for her safety, or her life, is the day I will say we're a civilized society."

"But, hasn't it gotten any better?"

"Over the centuries, yes. In my lifetime, no. As matter of fact, recently it's gotten worse."

"Yeah, in our current political atmosphere politicians seem to be getting elected on baseless or minor social issues which they use to try to push us back into the 1950s."

"Exactly. They focus on restructuring our society, pushing women out of positions of power and out of social view while the wealthy kill the economic power of the middle class. It's moving slowly, but it is happening." Sarah was slowly shaking her head as she finished her statement.

"Yes . . .You always inspire me. You make me think outside

my box. Thank you. Everything you have said I will research and write about. Thank you." Sarah nodded her head as she sipped her tea.

Mike watched her. He thought about how amazing she was. She viewed the world from so many different perspectives. She'd always had the ability to spin Mike's thoughts from a narrow path to a broader understanding. *She will do well.* Mike thought and then, "Excuse me, Mr. Smith?" A voice from beside the table caught Mike's attention.

"Oh, hey Elizabeth. I was just talking with–"

"I just wanted to say hi. Sorry I took a chance. You're probably working with a client. I'll see you another time."

"Wait, no, this is my daughter. She's actually teaching me. Sarah, Elizabeth. Elizabeth, my daughter Sarah."

"Quite pleased to meet you." She took Sarah's hand.

"Likewise."

"Well, I saw you and thought I would just come up and say hi."

"I'm glad you did. Would you like to join us with a cup of tea?"

"No thanks. I was on my way to the festival happening in the park and like I said, saw you."

"Well, I'm glad you did. As I said, any time you see me. How are you?"

"I'm doing quite well. Anyway, nice to see you and thank you for your guidance the other day. I'm sure I'll see you again. Nice to meet you Sarah. By the way, what are you teaching to the master?"

"I don't know that I'm a master." Mike stated.

"We were talking about how a woman has to watch her back, sadly even as a little girl, for all her life. Mostly against certain men."

"Oh, yeah, mostly men. Did you mention also watching out for previous relationships? A lot of women have been hurt, disfigured, or even killed because of disgruntled ex-partners or men pursuing unwanted attention."

"Well, there's more for your research, Dad."

"Also, Mr. Smith, do you know what the leading cause of death for pregnant women in the US is?" Elizabeth asked.

"Birthing complications?"

"No. In the US it's their 'intimate partners', as a search engine's AI puts it."

"Oh. I see. Sarah, you're right, we do seem to be going backwards."

"Mr. Smith, have you read the memoir, 'The Chronology of Water' by, Lidia Yuknavitch"?

"No."

"You should read it. Anyway, I'm going to head up to the park. Again, nice to meet you, Sarah."

"Wait, you're heading up to the art festival, what did you buy?" Sarah asked, referring to Elizabeth's bags.

"Uhm, just some pottery I liked."

"Pottery, I love ceramics. What did you get?"

"Uhm, there's these pieces I've always wanted from Joyce Maclan of the Art District." She showed them to Sarah.

"I love Joyce's work. Here, look what I picked up." Sarah showed her a bowl she bought from the gallery next to the kids' performing art center on Sebastopol Ave.

"Oh, I like that. Nice."

"Hey, I'll walk with you up to Juilliard Park. Dad?"

"Go! I'm fine. You guys have a good time. We'll catch up later. It's nice to see you, Elizabeth."

"You too, Mr. Smith."

"Please, call me Mike."

"Okay, Mike." Mike gave a small nod. The girls picked up their bags and were soon walking and talking like old friends. Mike thought, *Things guide us in ways that we don't understand. I think those two are going to be good friends.* He smiled as he got up. He picked up the cups and brought them into the restaurant. The buss tray was full, so he took them to the entrance of the kitchen and handed them to a waitperson. She thanked him. He picked up the latest copy of the Gazette. The front page was about the art festival going on this weekend. As he glanced at it, he walked out of Sisters. He looked in the direction that the girls had walked and froze. Just above the "Art Alley" street sign the two girls were talking to the man in white.

"Hey!" He yelled. They didn't hear him. He checked his surroundings and hurried across the street. He looked up and they were still talking. If he walked quickly maybe he could finally meet this mysterious man.

Wait! Why is he talking with my daughter? Mike thought. *Wait! Since they are talking, he must be real.* That gave Mike a sense of relief. He had been wondering if that earlier encounter was something he had imagined. He picked up his pace.

"Hey mister?" A young boy, looking distressed, had stopped him.

"Yeah?"

"Sorry, sir, you look nice, and I'm lost." Mike looked at the boy. He clearly needed some help, something that Mike would never refuse.

"Okay, okay, let's go into the Arts Center here. Maybe we could get you to Security. Okay?"

"I'm kinda scared."

"It's all right. I'll help you, c'mon." They walked into the gallery. Luck was with Mike. Because it was a busy festival there was a security guard right as they walked in. Mike looked for the guard's badge.

"Hey, whenever you find yourself in a scary situation and you need help, and your parents aren't with you, look for someone with an official looking badge." Mike told the young boy as he pointed at the guard. He looked for a name on the badge.

"Uhm, Lawrence, this young boy says his parents are lost. Can you help him find them."

"Yes, I have a report of some parents looking for a youngster. Are you William?"

"Yes, can you help me?" The boy seemed about to cry.

"Of course, that's my job. Thank you, sir, for finding him. His parents are deeply worried."

"So, you got this."

"Yes."

"See, William, they have found your lost parents." William's eyes started to tear. "Hey, you got a lollipop or something for him?" Mike asked the guard.

"I do. William, right over here, choose whatever you like." Lawrence had pointed to a bowl of candies near the front door. He finished talking on his radio and then to Mike, "Thank you again. His parents are on the way."

"Great. I was on my way to see my daughter, so, if you don't need me, I'm going to go find her."

"You're good. Thanks again for helping the boy."

"Hey William, don't let your parents wonder off again."

"I promise." Mike gave the kid a thumbs up, smiled and then left. He made his way back to the sidewalk and looked toward the park. The girls were almost there and, of course, the man in white was nowhere to be seen. Mike nearly ran as he caught up with the girls.

"Hey you guys." The girls turned toward him as he got close and took a moment to catch his breath.

"That guy you were talking to, all in white, what did he want?"

"He asked us if we knew of a good place to eat. We told him about Sisters, but when we pointed to it, he said 'thanks' and went into the park," Sarah said.

"Yeah, it was kinda weird." Elizabeth said with a shrug.

"That was it? That was all he said?"

"Yeah, Dad. You, okay?"

"I'm okay. It's just that we had an odd encounter about a week ago. I was hoping to talk with him."

"Well, he's in the park." Sarah pointed.

"Yeah, uh, somehow, I think he's probably already gone, like he did before. I think I'll just head home and get some after-therapy rest. Remember we're shopping at the grocery store in Healdsburg this Sunday at 3pm."

"I know. I'll be there."

"Okay. You girls have a fun time at the festival. I'm gonna go back to my house."

"Rest sounds good. See you Sunday. Oh, and love ya." Sarah gave him a quick hug and then walked with Elizabeth into the park.

"Love you back," Mike said as she walked away. He watched them for a couple of seconds and then turned toward his house.

He was standing behind one of the vendors' canopies as he watched Mike leave. He knew he wanted to speak with the man that called himself Mr. Smith. He had attended a couple of Mike's seminars about two years ago. He pulled off his white hat and pushed back his blond hair. Then the man in white thought to himself, *I know there's something I have to say to him, yet it's not revealing itself, so far...* He shook his head slightly and put his hat back on. With a sigh he turned and walked out of the park toward the downtown mall. He knew, at some point, they would meet.

CHAPTER SIX

Saturday, thankfully, was uneventful. Late Sunday morning he was finishing his cup of coffee while scrolling through the news on his phone. Shaking his head he thought, *some heartless jerk in Washington said, "The problem with Western Democracies is that they have too much empathy."* Mike looked out his window toward Julliard Park and saw a homeless man and his dog making their way to a sunny area of the park. He set his bag next to a park bench and then lay across the long bench seat. His dog obediently lay down next to the man's bag.

Mike watched for a bit and then thought, *There's not enough empathy. Politicians in DC live in a bubble. They have security, government health care, and those in gerrymandered districts are secure for life. They've completely lost connection with those they're supposed to represent.* He shook his head again. He looked out to the man and his dog. He watched as the more fortunate people changed paths to deliberately avoid the homeless man on the bench.

He rinsed out the empty coffee cup and set it on the side of the kitchen sink. It was noon. The day was getting away from him. He was to meet with his daughters at the Healdsburg grocery store to shop for their stay out by Lake Sonoma. That was a few hours from now. He looked out at the homeless man lying on a bench in the sun. He lightly shook his head again as he walked away from the window.

"I have a little time for research." Mike said to himself as he made his way to his office. The startling facts that Sarah and Elizabeth had expressed, in a very personal way, were still on his mind. He knew about it, based on previous research, but now he felt a need to dig further into the facts. He clicked on a saved address on his bookmark bar. The Child Crime Prevention & Safety Center (CCP) was one of the many resources Mike had bookmarked–a good website for specific and general information about childhood abductions in the US. According to the CCP there were 840,000 missing children reports filed nearly every year. Most of the reports were determined by law enforcement to be inaccurate or resolved. More than half the legitimate reports were family abductions, which are often determined not to be as dangerous to the child, and eventually get resolved. *Still, there is danger, as the officials in Child Protective Service and law enforcement I have worked with knew.* Mike thought while he shook his head.

Based on reports he saw, and the professionals he worked with, many of these missing kids eventually turned out to be runaways. Unfortunately, nearly three fourths of these are female. Most of these girls are between the ages of ten and eighteen. Nearly half of them are running away from physically abusive families. They are the ones that have the greatest risk of becoming homeless. Somewhere between 7% and 17% of them, depending on the year, are or will become pregnant. Aside from physical abuse, approximately 38% of the runaways are escaping emotional abuse and 17% percent are running away from sexual abuse.

Then he clicked on another excellent website for stats and facts, the National Center for Missing & Exploited Children, (NCMEC). They are a non-profit organization that has worked remotely with various state and federal law enforcement agencies. According to their site they helped with 29,568 cases of missing children in 2024 with a success rate of over 90% recovered. Unfortunately, even with their high recovery rate, they are also showing that the reports of sextortion are on the rise. Sextortion is the use of emotional, physical or mind-altering drugs to force someone into paid sexual acts. In 2024 the NCMEC reported over 100 incidents of paid sextortion per day. Since 2021 the NCMEC has proven that the suicides of 36 young boys were directly related to sextortion. Although all these stats are clear and well documented, many people find them inconvenient and turn the other way.

Mike wrote a few notes and again shook his head. The facts speak for themselves. Plus, the fact that some states are stupidly rolling back their child labor laws. In one such state some children can work with unlimited time restrictions, even up to eleven o'clock at night on school days. Instead of the state helping their parents with minimum wage increases, it has set up many of its kids for potential abuse by employers or the dangerous late-night walk home. *Sometimes, politicians, trying to look like they're pro-business, just look stupid,* Mike thought.

That triggered the stat that Elizabeth shared on Friday: the fact that the number one cause of death for pregnant women is their partners. Race and location skew the facts, but, sadly, it's true that in the United States, some mothers-to-be, need to be wary of their significant other.

Mike glanced at his phone. "Ah, time to get ready to go." Time seemed to pass quickly when he did research. He jotted down a few more notes. He glanced at his calendar and was reminded that his next seminar was a week and a half after the family gathering. He placed that in the back of his mind and then shut down the computer and headed toward the garage, but, before he left, he walked across the park to the man on the bench and gave him a twenty-dollar bill.

It was around two o'clock on Sunday afternoon. Traffic was moderate. He would easily make it up to Healdsburg in half an hour. He thought about Elizabeth, Sarah's new friend, again. She was obviously intelligent, had empathy and a confident personality. It struck him how interesting it was that there are a few people who can, without therapy, eventually leave their negative childhood experiences behind. They can find the confidence to function in society as themselves. With a sudden understanding, an epiphany wrapped in self-awareness, they tell themselves, "This is not the way I want to live," and make a life empowering adjustment. Even though she was in therapy, Elizabeth struck him as one of those people. *Hmm, she might be an interesting partner at some of the seminars.* That thought gave him a smile.

He made his way to Healdsburg and, since he had a few minutes, got an iced coffee at the local coffee shop. He drove up the street to the store and parked in its lot. He saw Rose's Tahoe SUV. Not surprised, as she was always on time or early, he made his way into the store. Rose, with her baby, Weston, attached to her front, was talking to her daughter, Walker.

"Honey, we're shopping for our stay at the ranch house. I promise we'll get you some treats after we're done shopping." Walker had her arms across her chest and a grumpy look on her face. Clearly, she didn't agree. Then Rose saw Mike.

"Dad!" Mike was just the distraction she needed. Walker turned to see Mike and then, "Grandpa Mike!" The four-year-old scooted over to give him a hug.

"Hey little one, good to see you." He returned the hug.

"Yep. Are we shopping for the ranch house?"

"Yes, we are." He ran his hand across the top of her head.

"Hi, sweetheart." He gave Rose and the infant a hug.

"Good timing, Dad." She smiled, referring to her battle with her daughter.

"So, I see. Is Sarah here?"

"Not yet. You know she can be fashionably late."

"Yeah, I know."

"Hey guys. Look at you!" As if on cue Sarah walked into the store with open arms as Walker ran up to her.

"You've gotten so big." She gave the little one a squeeze.

"Yep, and mom says you're getting old." Sarah laughed.

"Walker! We were talking about birthdays." Rose laughed and then offered an explanation, an excuse, for her daughter's comment.

"I don't care. Someday you're going to get older too." She spoke to Walker with a smile.

"I can't wait. Then I can get some treats whenever I want." Walker spoke first to Sarah and then to her mom.

"Yes, you can, sweetheart, but don't be in a hurry to grow up. Take your time. Enjoy being little. Being grown-up can also be tough. Just ask your mom," Sarah lightly admonished the youngster. Walker looked over at her mom.

"What your aunt said."

Mike just absorbed the light family banter, and then, "All right, let's get started. I was thinking we need food for daily consumption and then something for a big family dinner."

"Oh, I invited Elizabeth. I hope that's okay?"

"And who's Elizabeth?" Rose asked Sarah.

"A new, really good friend. Dad knows her."

"Yes, I do. She's okay, she's very much like your sister." Mike said to Rose.

"Great, the more the merrier. What does that actually mean, like my sister?"

"Well–" Sarah started to explain, but Mike interrupted.

"C'mon guys, let's get this done so we can bring stuff out to the ranch."

"Okay, let's go! Grandpa Mike, you push." Walker climbed onto the front of the shopping cart.

"Gotcha, little one. Okay you guys, let's just go down each aisle and see what we need." Mike pushed the cart toward the meat department.

"Everybody's already had lunch, right?" Sarah asked.

"We have." Rose answered.

"So have I." It was Mike.

"Hey, where's Tyler?" Sarah asked Rose.

"He's cleaning up the place we are staying at. We plan to be at the ranch tomorrow. By the way, I claim first picks on our rooms."

"Aw, I was going to say that to you as we shopped." Sarah smiled. "I get it. You have a family." Sarah gestured toward the kids. Rose nodded.

"Hey, shall we get some steaks for tomorrow? I know Tyler likes to barbecue." It was Mike.

"Yes, but we need to include some good healthy greens, like a salad and side dish."

"I like broccoli!" Walker interjected.

"Me too! You're so smart." Mike said to her, with a big smile.

They had ordered some proteins from the butcher and made their way around a few more grocery aisles. Four-month-old Weston was starting to fuss a little as they reached the paper goods aisle. Rose started to bounce the baby a bit, while Walker kept saying, "It's okay Weston. It's okay..." Mike was looking at getting some paper plates and such, so they wouldn't have to constantly be washing dishes when Sarah stopped him.

"Dad, look!" Sarah gestured toward the end of the aisle. There, moving to the right across the aisle, was the man in white. Mike froze, and then to himself, "This is getting weird. Hey, mister!" Mike bellowed as the man crossed past the aisle and disappeared. Mike started walking fast and called again, "Hey mister."

"Dad?" Sarah called to him.

Mike got to the end of the paper goods and turned right. He was gone for about ten seconds and came back into the girls' view, deeply puzzled, hands out and shaking his head. The man had already vanished. Mike, clearly distressed, turned and headed in the opposite direction.

"I think we need to calm Dad down. Dad! Dad!" Sarah told Rose and then yelled for Mike, as she followed him.

"Grandpa Mike!" Walker shouted, trying to do her part. Except she ran in the opposite direction toward where they entered the aisle. That stopped Sarah.

"Rose?"

"I got Walker. You find Dad. Walker, wait for me." Rose called.

Sarah watched as Rose hurried after Walker. The shopping cart stood by itself. For a second she thought, *"I can't just leave it there.* She shook her head at the thought and turned to go find Mike. She got to the back of the aisle and looked in both directions. Neither man was visible. On a lark she moved to her right. She looked down a couple of aisles, but there was no sign of that blond haired man. She quickly turned and went in the opposite direction. She looked down each aisle, but no Mike. Finally, she made her way to the produce area at the end of the store. There was her dad leaning against one of the dry tables. He looked confused and, in a way, defeated. Concerned, she hurried up to him. He looked at her for a second and then looked away.

"Dad?" She was worried. He just stared. "Dad?" She touched his left shoulder. "Are you alright?" Mike looked at her for about five seconds.

"I just saw Kevin." He barely spoke as he looked off to the right.

"You what!" She grabbed both his shoulders to make him look at her. "You what?"

"I just saw my brother."

"Dad, Dad, Kevin's been gone for nearly thirty years. You didn't just see your brother."

"I did, for a second. He was standing right there, at the end of this table." Mike gestured to his left.

"Dad–"

"Listen, I know what I saw. It may be the tough time I'm having at the moment, but he was right there. He looked back at me, smiled and then walked around the table to where I couldn't see him. I followed around and there was this young man, he looked a bit like Kevin, but it wasn't what I saw. The young man looked at me like I was crazy. . .maybe I am. He walked away from this crazy man that looked at him like he was a ghost. I know what I saw, and I know I'm not hallucinating."

"Dad, Kevin took his own life. He's no longer with us."

"I know. He's been on my mind a lot as I am going through this emotionally tough time right now. It's possible that I just wanted to see him, that I would love to see him one more time; just to let him know I wish I had been there…"

"Dad, you know he had lost his way. He was an abuser and a criminal. You know that is true. Not to say he deserved to die, but it was his decision to lead the life he did."

"I know, but I also know how close we were as kids. He– Wait!" Mike stood straight and looked to the other end of the store. The man in white, as Mike called him, with a bag in his hands, was exiting. This time Mike stopped himself from running after him.

"Dad?" Sarah touched her dad's cheek to pull his gaze toward her. "Dad?"

"It's all right, honey. I have this feeling that we're supposed to meet, but it's going to have to happen naturally. I'm done. Let's get this shopping experience over." Mike forced a reassuring smile to Sarah and started walking back to the cart.

The rest of the shopping was uneventful, though Mike was deep in thought and had very little to say. They got the groceries settled in the house and sat around the front porch for a few minutes. After a bit Rose and her kids left. Sarah stayed a little longer, mostly to see how Mike was doing.

"I need to leave pretty soon Dad. What are your plans?"

"I think I'm going to stay here tonight."

"Do you need to let the owners know?"

"I'll tell Alonzo tomorrow."

"You going to be okay?"

"I'll be fine, honey. You head back. I'll see you tomorrow."

"What time?"

"As I told Rose, whenever you get up and packed, head on over."

"All right, Dad. See you tomorrow. Love you."

"Love you too." Sarah gave him a quick hug and a smile and then got into her car and left.

Mike sat on the porch. Dusk was coming and with it the mosquitoes. He doused himself with some deet-free repellent and sat as the sun set and the sky turned to dusk. The house was surrounded by a forest. It wasn't long before he heard the quiet sound of the crepuscular bat wings fluttering around. He remembered the battles he used to wage trying to keep those mammals out of the nooks and crannies of the house. Still, he thought of them as an amazing evolutionary experiment. They exist to eat the annoying flying bugs that prey on humans and the house. He sat there deep in thought when he had this feeling of being watched. He looked off to his left and there, not much more than thirty feet, and on the other side of the fence, was a very large mountain lion.

He slowly sat up straight to stare at the puma that was staring at him. He didn't feel any fear. Also, the front door was just five feet away. To him it was a fascinating experience. Usually, you don't see a wild lion like this. The puma was sitting and looking at him, his tail swishing about, which did make Mike a little nervous. The fence was about seven feet tall; an easy jump for a mountain lion. The animal suddenly set his gaze further down the creek. *Probably sees dinner. Well, at least it's not me.* Mike thought.

"You know I'm not supposed to see you." Mike said to the animal. As if to reply the big cat gave a low growl. Mike wasn't sure if it was meant for him or whatever the puma saw in the creek ditch. Mike decided he would make his way into the house. He walked without incident and closed the front door behind him. Still, he was curious about that brazen cat. He knew that it was unusual to see a wild mountain lion up so close. He stood behind a curtain where he could watch the cat. It still stared at the general front porch area where Mike had been. Then the cat looked back down into the creek and crouched. With one leap it cleared the fence and slowly walked along the side of the house and into the back yard. It was a magnificent example of elegance, beauty and danger. It made its way to the end of the back fence. Then in one graceful leap it was over that fence and into the foliage. Mike watched it all in amazement.

"How fortunate. It must have been watching us when we got here earlier and then, with a little bit of good timing, it let me see him. He's a big cat. Interesting, life, the universe, deities, whatever you want to call it, bring joyful and amazing events together that are there for us to experience, to make us just a bit more aware of the natural world around us. We just have to be willing to see and accept that moment." Mike said to himself. He knew he would not forget this.

He made his way into bed, turned on the laptop, but then fell into a deep sleep.

CHAPTER SEVEN

The family began to arrive Monday after 11am. Mike had a decent sleep, though he did have another nightmare. This one seemed to be back under his control. Though no matter when he had these bad dreams, they were always fearful. Yet, for the first time recently, in this nightmare he managed to morph from the child in an abusive and scary situation into the adult Mike. He remembered the oppressive feeling of being held down and the fear, but suddenly he was an adult confronting his abusers. It was odd. As an adult he stood up, the darkness fell away, and the perpetrators were gone. There was a child's teddy bear lying on a cot-like bed in his dream. He grabbed that stuffed bear by the throat, and slammed it against a wall, and started screaming, "Who are you! Who the fuck are you!"

As he yelled and violently shook the stuffed animal, across the dream-bear flashed a series of different faces. Some he recognized, like his grandmother and stepfather, but the rest were unfamiliar. He kept banging it against the wall as he yelled. The intense hatred and violence he raged against that dream-bear was more than he had ever felt. All he wanted to do was hurt someone. That also scared him. The sheer ferocity of his anger at the projected faces woke him up. Yet it felt cathartic. After a bit he went back to sleep, but in the morning, upon waking, he had a sense of relief. He had managed to become the adult.

The kids were arguing over which rooms they were going to call their own, but in a familial way. As the laughter and friendly jabs were settling it was clear that Rose and Tyler would have one room with the baby and Walker would get her own room. Sarah wanted and did get the upstairs room, where she had spent a good deal of her youth. During the kids' bantering, Mike made his way out to the front porch. It was a sunny, mild late spring day in Sonoma County. The cherry trees had already blossomed and there were a lot of cherry buttons on the branches. It would be another few weeks before they were ripe.

"Hey Dad, I'm going to see Elizabeth later today, so don't plan on me for dinner." Sarah came out and sat down near Mike.

"You know honey, she's always welcome here. You can invite her over for dinner."

"I know. We made plans so I probably won't get back till late."

"I'll leave the door unlocked."

"Thanks. How are you doing? Anymore Kevin sightings?"

"No. Hopefully that was a fluke. This morning, I feel fine."

"Well, I still think you should contact your therapist and talk about what you saw."

"Thank you. I have an appointment for early Wednesday to meet with Dr. Lowell."

"Oh, I'm so glad. And you know, following your own advice, you shouldn't have too much alcohol while you're in this healing place. I worry about you."

"I know honey, and I appreciate and love you all the more for that. It has been a struggle lately."

"Well, after talking with Elizabeth and hearing all the challenges she faced, and is still battling, I have a lot more understanding of what you've gone through. Still, you have done everything that any responsible parent could have done to keep Rose and me safe and strong throughout our childhood. Considering your grandmother and your stepfather's history of abuse, I thank you for that."

"I love you. And my goal as a parent was to give you, and Rose, what I thought you needed to be strong and confident enough to deal with anything.

"After Kevin committed suicide, the surviving siblings came together. We talked about the family's sad history, or as much as we knew of it, and as we later learned that pattern of abuse was part of my family's secret, my family's cyclic history of abuse. We decided the abuse ended with us.

"Apparently, back in the day, and according to the many sources I researched, when it came to abuse, it was a 'family issue', not something the authorities would be involved in. The number of children who died or were forever damaged because of local law enforcement's unwillingness to help is beyond understanding. Why would you not want to help a child?"

"Perhaps they did, but their abilities to help were hampered by the lack of any clear laws. Thankfully, that has changed."

"Yes, but it still happens. As we know from Elizabeth and many others I see in my seminars. Elizabeth said she is not consuming any alcohol, does that appear to be true?"

"You know, Dad, I don't truly understand the flaws of those that have been so terribly abused as a child. I just know it happens. I have so much compassion for those that are trying to put that PTSD behind them."

"I'm glad you don't share that experience."

"I haven't seen Liz drinking any alcohol, but I can see on her face, when she looks at certain alcoholic drinks, that she must have liked those at one time."

"I think everyone who has experienced such severe trauma finds something to numb the pain, their shame and their inability to be what they perceive to be normal. They look at the media and their friends and think, 'That's normal. Why can't I be that way?' Some do find their way without therapy, usually at a price, maybe by burying a part of them they don't like, a piece of their soul, or by creating a dominant personality, making them believe that they are in control. At least so they think. To heal you must walk through the PTSD, through that angst." Mike was talking to Sarah but also thinking aloud.

"Yeah . . .As I got older, and perhaps wiser, I understood more about you as a man and as a dad and, now that I am a grown woman, my mom too, of course." Sarah mused.

"I can't think of any child that's ever said, 'My parents were perfect.'" That made her laugh.

"Well, just so you know, you guys definitely weren't perfect." She smiled.

"I know. But it was our goal to keep you and Rose safe. Looking at you and Rose now, I think we did okay."

"Yes, you both did, you did your best. Thank you." Sarah stood, "Okay. It's getting close to one, so I'm going to head out, run some errands and then meet with Elizabeth. Don't worry about me for dinner. I'll see you later tonight."

"Sounds good. Like I said, I'll leave the door unlocked and the light on. Have a good time with your friend."

"Will do!"

Mike watched as his daughter did a brisk walk to her car. She would be 38 on her next birthday. He thought about all the years he spent watching over her and how tough it was to see her head off to Europe for college at seventeen. *It's all part of the great circle. You give them roots and then you watch as they spread their wings. As far as I'm concerned, when it comes to being a father, to the best of my abilities, it was one of the most rewarding experiences I had.* Mike's thought brought a smile to his face.

He checked his phone; it was a little past one. The thought of lunch crossed his mind. He went back into the house. Walker was sitting at the piano. She plucked a couple of keys and then started giggling.

"Grandpa Mike! Momma's making lunch. Do you wanna turn?" She asked, referring to the piano.

"Not right now, sweetheart. You play. I'm going to help your mom."

"Do you know how to play?"

"No, I don't, but my friend, Lee, does know how to play. Ask her when you see her."

"I will." She then ran her fingers across the keys, which started her to giggle again. Mike watched her for a moment. Like all healthy, secure young children, she was full of life. It was a joy to watch her.

"That's beautiful!" He said to her cacophony. She simply

said, "Yep." He laughed and walked into the kitchen.

"She's going to be a concert pianist." Mike said with a smile to Rose.

"Oh my, that's going to take some lessons." Rose laughed.

"Yeah, the hard part is getting her to practice."

"Yeah, I remember."

"Well, you rarely, if ever, hear an adult say, 'I wish my parents hadn't forced me to practice.'" Rose had tried to play a violin, but her mom and Mike never found a way to convince her to commit to her daily violin drills. Though now, as an adult, she really didn't care. "What can I do to help with lunch?"

"I got it, Dad. Just making some sandwiches. Do you want chips and lemonade with yours?"

"Yeah, sounds good. What are your plans for today?"

"We are going to take a walk up to the top of the ridge overlooking Lake Sonoma."

"With the baby?"

"Yeah, he's only around fourteen pounds. We'll trade carrying him in the front carrier. The path is generally good."

"Sounds like a good hike. One of you should carry something in your hands. I don't think the puma is a threat, probably more curious, but still, better to be careful."

"I know, you mentioned it." Just then Mike's phone rang. He pulled it from its holder.

"Oh, it's Lee. I'm going to get this, honey." Mike said as he walked away. Walker was still plucking on the piano, so Mike stepped out.

"Good afternoon," Mike chimed.

"Same to you. I just finished with my last client and I know we are getting together on Friday at the ranch, but I thought, if you have time today, we'd do a little wine tasting."

"You know, that sounds good, but if it's okay with you I'd rather get a nice hike in, while the weathers' still moderate. What do you think?"

"Okay by me. Where would you like to hike?"

"Well, there's the Porterfield Creek Park in Cloverdale or

around Lake Sonoma?"

"Let's do Lake Sonoma. It's a better chance to view some wildlife."

"Oh yeah, rattlesnakes, puma and wild boar."

"Oh my."

"Haha, very funny. How about the Overlook Trail?"

"Yeah, we've had some nice walks and talks on that trail in the past. Shall I meet you there?"

"How about I meet you at the ranch, and we go in one car?"

"Okay, looking forward to it."

"Great. See you soon." Mike gave her the gate code, disconnected and put the phone back in its case holder.

"Hey Dad, sandwich."

"Thank you, Rose. Hmm, it sounds like the piano concert is over."

"She's eating. We're going to head up the trail right after. Can I get you anything else before we leave?"

"No thanks, sweetheart. Lee is coming over and we're going to take a hike at the lake."

"Oh, good. I like Lee. Maybe we'll be here when you guys get back. It'll be nice to see her."

"Yeah, she's a good one."

"Hm-hm, you should remember that." Rose said as she walked back into the house. Mike smiled.

As Mike finished the lunch Rose made for him, the kids and grandkids all geared up, made their way toward the back gate. Mike walked with them through the gate and to the bridge he built many years ago. He wanted to see how it looked. It was a simple design. A couple of 18"x18" redwood beams spanning the creek about twenty feet, covered with composite decking and a rail on one side. Because of the span it had a small bounce to it, which Walker found to be a lot of fun. They said, "See ya later" to each other and Mike walked back to the house, just as Lee pulled down the driveway. She parked near the garage and was getting out as Mike approached.

"Hey there, nice to see you."

"The same," she said as she closed the car door and gave Mike a friendly hug. "So, which car should we drive in?"

"Doesn't matter. Mine is pointing out, so, we can take my car. I've got a cold flask of water in the house. Let me grab it and we'll scoot."

"Sounds good." She walked with Mike into the house. "So, my friend, how are you?" Mike smiled at the question. Between Dr. Lowell, Lee, and his girls, that question has come up quite a few times. It wasn't a bad thing. It was gratifying. He knew the inquiries were sincere. He was prepared with a pat answer, then caught himself. It was Lee. He knew she truly did care about how he was doing.

"Truth to tell, I'm a mixed bag. I thought I saw my brother in the grocery store yesterday. It was someone that looked like him, but it reveals to me how much the abusive past is on my mind lately."

"To the extent that you may be hallucinating?"

"Are you asking me as a therapist?"

"You know my feelings about that. You have a counselor, a good one. No, I'm asking because I care for you." They were walking toward Mike's car. "I love you as a friend."

"And, maybe, as a lover?" Mike said that, trying to be sly.

"We tried that. Remember? There were some sweet moments, but you said you weren't ready." Lee gave a knowing smile. Mike smiled too as he opened the door for her.

"I remember." There was a certain sadness in his response. He closed her door and scurried over to the driver's side.

"So, how are you? How was your session?"

"As you know, sometimes they're tough. This one was a bit anyway. But I'm doing well. Thanks for asking." She gently touched his arm.

"Thanks for being my friend," he said as he headed up the driveway. Lee smiled. They drove ten minutes or so to the lake in silence.

CHAPTER EIGHT

Mike had parked up near the tower overlooking Lake Sonoma. They climbed to the top of the structure and spent a few minutes looking out at the marina, the dam and one of the lake's channels.

"Remember the time we kayaked from the marina up that one leg of the lake?" Lee asked as she pointed to her left.

"Yeah, I remember you started singing, 'Don't rock the boat.' And tipped us over." Mike smiled at the memory.

"Mmm-hmm, as I remember you helped with the rocking."

"Well, yeah, I mean, it is a catchy song." Lee laughed at Mike's response.

"Fortunately, we were close enough to shore to drag the kayak into shallow water," she managed to say through her chuckles.

"Yeah… That was a fun day. Shall we get on with our hike?"

"Sure." They started down the stairs and headed toward the trail. "Mike, one of my kids has a bass boat they're trying to sell. I think I'm going to buy it. I mean I'll look into all the stuff I need, like insurance and the correct hitch and such, but if I get it, we should look at a week off from work and take a trip around the lake. There's fifty miles of shoreline and I'd say, ninety percent of it is only accessible by boat."

"A week? That's a lot of prep. There's food, camping, fishing, a lot. Wait, are you asking me to go with you on a weeklong date?" Mike smiled.

"I guess you could call it that."

"Hmm, I think I'd like that."

"Platonic, of course."

"Well, let's see how we feel after a couple of glasses of wine," Mike said with a smile. Lee returned the smile and gave his arm a hug. They were just starting on the trail when Mike grabbed Lee and stopped her. There, about five feet in front of them, was a fat rattlesnake sunning on a flat stone in their pathway. Had he not seen it, they would have stepped on it. They stepped back as the snake curled and shook its tail. It was a good-sized snake. It was interesting to Mike that as it rattled its tail so hard and fast it sounded like a hissing water leak from an irrigation pipe. They looked at it as they backed further away.

"Well, I guess we're not going that way." Lee stated the obvious.

"Right."

"That was a big rattler. I'm glad you saw it," she said as they headed in the opposite direction.

"Yeah, me too." They walked in silence for a bit. "You know, I never told my stepfather how much I hated him."

"A new subject, are you sure you want to talk about that now?"

"It's on my mind. Lately, it's all on my mind."

"I mean, I get it. You've been through a lot recently. What's on your mind?"

"The abuse, the guilt, my brother, the whole ugly mess. You know my history as well as anyone. So, yeah, a lot, especially that piece of scum."

"Did you ever tell him you loved him?"

"I didn't have that feeling anywhere in these bones. Interesting though, both Kevin and Arlene did tell him they loved him. I guess they were trying to get some love in return, instead of abuse. I know as adults, they both hated him. Hate is probably not a strong enough word for how they felt. No, I never said that to him, but I also never told him how much I flat-out hated him."

"Hate is a powerful emotion."

"Yeah, I know."

"When do you see your therapist again?"

"Wednesday morning."

"May I make a suggestion?"

"Of course."

"Talk about your brother."

"I think that's her intention. She had said earlier that my brother would be a separate session."

"Leaning a bit on my professional experience, but mostly as someone who deeply cares about you, I think it would be beneficial for you to discuss the fact that you and Kevin grew in separate directions."

"I know that intellectually. We were so close as kids. I get emotional, as you have seen over the years, but somewhere I have this hurt that sometimes, like now, overwhelms me because I wasn't there, not only to help my siblings, but also for Kevin, when he shot himself," Mike said quietly, then fell into silence. Lee walked along Mike's side, trying to give him some time. The Overlook trail lived up to its name. At one point the trail opened to a view of the western part of Dry Creek Valley. Mike and Lee stopped and looked at the green vineyards that dominated the valley.

"It's beautiful." Lee's voice was soft. Mike nodded. The spring vines seemed to glow in the afternoon sun. Mike was always fascinated by how humans saw color. Like most humans he could see variegated shades of green among different and similar plants. He knew green was the color wavelength that was reflected off the leaves. They were more likely to be the colors red and blue; but we, as the primates called humans, aren't able to see the actual colors, we can only see the color reflected, which is green. It's like the leaves are pretending to be something that they are not. *How human of you,* Mike thought. Deep in thought he started back down the trail. Lee felt him leave her side and quickly caught up. "You okay?"

"Yeah." Another minute of silence. "We were inseparable, Kevin and me. We went everywhere together. We climbed deep into the woods behind Building 8 in the Beardsley Terrace, often called the projects, climbing up to where the natural stone marble reached out of the earth and gifted us a place to sit.

"Kids at the projects, some like us, but mostly kids of color, were very poor. Some of the kids were also very cruel. The older ones in Building 7 and Building 8 used to have gang fights with knives and broken bottles. Kevin and I would hide our tiny selves in our apartment, occasionally sneaking a glance out of a window. It was a rough place to turn seven. That's where my mother met our soon to be abusive stepfather. It took a while, but the family finally ended up in a nicer area of the city. Still lower middle class, but safer.

"In that area we ran feral. We played and built hideaways among the various lots of a fading industrial area off Wells St., in Bridgeport, Connecticut. I still have dreams about that house.

"We'd visit the old lady at the top of our three-story rental and the huge darkish basement with a monstrous furnace guarding its center. We lived on the first floor. Funny, I don't remember the folks that lived on the second floor. I do remember my stepfather pounding our ceiling with a broom handle because he thought the people above our heads were too noisy. I think he just saw that on a Jackie Gleason show and thought he would mimic it. After all, everybody wanted to be like the families in the sitcoms of those days."

"Sounds like you and Kevin enjoyed that time of your life."

"We did. In one of the lots, we built a small area to sit in a tree, which we called a fort, and ate the ripe concord grapes that used to wind through the tree's branches. We chased flying grasshoppers, that were as big as my child hand. We ate wild, huge, purple beefsteak tomatoes that seemed to grow everywhere. We used to get gigantic cardboard boxes and slide down the hills in the summer and use our sleds in the winter. It was a good time. Though, underneath it all, was the abuse."

"I'm sorry."

"My stepfather was a sick man." He walked a little further in silence. They were getting closer to the end of the trail, which ran through a parking lot just a bit down the road from the tower. The choices were to exit there or go back the way they came, following the trail around to where they had seen the snake earlier. The snake was probably gone by now, but Mike didn't want to take a chance, so he led them to and through the lower car lot. From there they would walk up the road to their original parking area. He continued, "When I landed a job as a performer at Universal Studios, our young familytraveled to Florida to secure a home and show our Florida relatives our beautiful new baby, Sarah. It was a joyous occasion. I had landed a good performing arts job. Even my stepfather seemed happy and overwhelmed. Then he showed us who he really was." Mike shook his head as he remembered what he saw. Lee could see what looked like sadness on his face. It was sad, but also from a place of pure disgust. He kept clenching his teeth.

"Mike, what happened?"

"It was a normal, innocuous family gathering. We were in a public park, as I recall it was the Lower Wekiva River Preserve, Wekiva being the Native American name for the Saint John's River. Anyway, my stepfather was just above me, arms folded and casually leaning against a tree. It fell upon me to change our baby's diaper. I pulled off Sarah's dirty diaper and reached over for a clean one. As I turned back toward my daughter, in the corner of my eye, I saw my messed-up stepfather crouched like an animal looking at my baby girl. He had leaned in toward her, still a few feet away, but had what I can only describe as a maniacal look on his face. I had never seen this look on a human. It was the look of a predatory animal ready to pounce on its prey. It was savage. He took a couple of steps toward her and my brain immediately went into a defense mode. I had to protect my child. I was ready to meet his attack and kill if necessary. I never had those thoughts before and, thankfully, never had them again." Mike stopped as he recalled the horrific experience.

"My God," Lee said, partially to herself.

"Yeah, so, he was crouched, focused on my semi-naked girl and I was prepared to meet him. I was done with his bullshit. But when he saw the way I was looking back at him he stopped. Then he metamorphosed like a chameleon. As he saw me, ready to do whatever I needed to do to protect Sarah, his body suddenly started shaking, he mumbled something and shook his head so hard, his cheeks waggled. He quickly jumped back, folded his arms and assumed the same position, leaning back against the tree with a laid-back attitude. Just like he was when I started changing Sarah." Again, in his mind, Mike recalled the look in his stepfather's eyes. They walked in silence up toward the parking area.

"Then what happened?" Lee touched his shoulder.

"Eventually a few years later, and for many reasons, none good, we decided that we did not want our daughter to grow up in Florida. He asked us to take him back to California. We, of course, told him he could not come and live with us. He begged. I didn't give a damn. He would never, ever again be near my child. Then, there was my brother."

"What do you mean?"

"His abuse of my niece. The cycle of abuse. The kids he parented and left. The abusive family, where does it end?"

"It ends with you!" Lee stopped him as they reached their car. "It ended with you!" Mike nodded.

"Yes. It ended with us siblings. Still, sometimes, it tears me apart. Often when I least expect it."

"It's a horrible thing to live with. But you know, you and your sisters ended that horrible cycle of child abuse. Whether your kids know it or not, you are all heroes. Silent ones, still nevertheless a hero for your kids." Mike teared up. "Then what happened to your stepfather?"

"He went into one of those homes. He eventually lost his mind altogether. He started grabbing the nurses and such. They had to drug him to a point where he was comatose. He died in that state. I have no idea where they buried him, if they did. I honestly don't care"

"Is that the end of his sad story?"

"Yes and no. Years later my mother told my sister of a little girl's death that she believed was perpetrated by him."

"Wait, what?"

"My mother was older and had had a stroke a couple of years earlier and her cognitive abilities were questionable at this point. Anyway, she told my sister about an incident where my stepfather came home one night with the decapitated body of a young girl. She said that he had raped and killed her. She told my sister that she was forced to help bury the body in their backyard. She recalled how he acted like he was sad, remorseful, but still threatened to kill her if she didn't help. She also told my sister that she had asked where the head of the child's body was and he told her that he had tossed it into a paint can. Now, my mother had a tendency to take different stories, news, gossip and such, and then mesh those varied stories into a single incident. Still, when I think of how he looked at my half naked daughter, I wouldn't put it past him."

"Wait, this is a goddamn serious claim. Have you told the authorities?"

"Yes, of course. As soon as I heard this story from my sister, Lana, I immediately called the FBI's cold case number. I left a detailed message and my phone number and never heard back. I assumed they had already looked into it."

"Well, first of all, now that you have told me this, I am obligated to report it."

"I know that. Given what I just relayed to you, I would expect you to."

"Christ, I am so sorry. That you wear that story along with everything else I know, I'm so, so sorry."

"Yeah."

They were at Mike's car. He followed Lee to the passenger's side and opened the door for her. She smiled at him.

"And despite everything you're still a gentleman." Mike smiled. "You're a good man, Mike. Don't forget that. People try to be what they think is a good man or woman, but mostly they're just trying. You, you are that decent human being. People can see that. That's probably why so many love you. You just have to be yourself." Mike blushed.

"It's okay. You can accept the fact that you are loved."

"It's taken a long time to just be myself; to treat people with kindness. The way I would like to be treated. Sometimes it's hard."

"Sure, and that's true for almost everybody on this planet.

We all think we can be better or do better than we are. Ironically, most of us are doing the best we can. You okay for driving?"

"Yeah, I'm good. Lee, I appreciate you. You are loved too. Thank you for listening to me."

"Thank you for trusting me." She gave him a hug, then got into the car. Mike closed her door and walked over to the driver's side. They headed back to the ranch in silence. He parked just next to Lee's car. The kids had returned from their hike to the top of the world and were hanging around the front porch. Walker came up to the parked car and was tapping on the window. "Is that Miss Lee?" she asked as Mike opened the door.

"Yes, she is."

"She can play?" Walker seemed excited.

"Oh, my goodness. I told Walker that you know how to play the piano. She's going to want to hear you play. Sorry." Mike smiled as he spoke to Lee.

"Haha. Does she know Twinkle Twinkle Little Star?" Lee said as she chuckled.

"I'm sure she does."

"Well then, this is going to be fun. I hear you are a famous piano player, is that true?" Lee said to Walker as they headed toward the house with Walker in the lead.

"Yep!" Walker exclaimed.

"Great! I can't wait for you to help me with the keys."

"Yay. What are keys? Do we have to start a piano engine?" Lee laughed and then looked at Mike with a big smile. She turned back to Walker and they talked among themselves. Every now and then Lee's fingers would mimic a walk across the piano keys. Walker quickly followed with her hand motion.

Mike watched as the two walked into the house. Rose and Tyler were sitting on the front porch with drinks in hand. The baby was on a soft quilt on the porch next to Rose. She suddenly gave a huge laugh at something that Tyler said. Mike took it all in and smiled.

CHAPTER NINE

Tuesday for Mike was uneventful, for the most part. No nightmares plaguing the night before and just family gatherings throughout the day. Rose, Tyler, their kids and Sarah and Elizabeth took a short walk to the local winery next door. In the sun it was hot, summer was on its way and was reminding the family of the heat yet to come. Fortunately, a breeze made the shady areas comfortable. While the kids were away Mike walked the creek that made up the irrigation system. He knew it well since he was the one that had set the original piping. The two wells in the creek filled the 7500-liter tank that supplied yard and garden irrigation. Every now and then the piping required maintenance.

The family had a great day at the wine tasting and then just running around hooting and hollering in the backyard. Tyler and Walker were playing Wiffle Ball, and, of course Walker scored more runs than Tyler. Every now and then Zeus would grab one of the balls and run around while Walker gave chase. Elizabeth and Sarah chose to walk through the backfields into the magical lands of Sarah's youth. There was a tree-fort Mike had built for her years ago. It was basically a level piece of plywood laid across the branches of an old, familiar tree. It was crumbling, but Sarah wanted to show the spot to Elizabeth. Mike took great care to remind the two girls of the potential rattlesnakes in the area. Sarah took a moment to remind her dad that she already had taken it into consideration. Mike laughed. He knew she knew, but still, he couldn't help being dad.

As the day closed Mike sat on the front porch and listened to the beginning of the nighttime sounds watching the bats with their whispering wings fly around the property. Mike was always grateful to those flying hunters that ate the airborne mosquitoes and termites. It was a good day.

Wednesday was different. Mike got to the appointment with Dr. Lowell. At first it went well and then devolved into a difference between Mike's understanding of his brother's death and Dr. Lowell's understanding of Mike's feelings of culpability. He felt she tried a bit too hard to convince Mike that he shouldn't bear responsibility for Kevin's suicide.

"Why do you feel responsible for your brother's death? Did he not use your personal info to grift a credit card company into thinking it was you, when in actuality it was Kevin? Didn't he touch your niece inappropriately? Wasn't he responsible for babies around the country? Make me understand Mike, why you are feeling like you are somehow responsible for your brother's death?"

"I don't know, I mean I am not responsible for Kevin's death. Yes, he used my personal info to gain credit cards. Yes, he had lied to his partners and because of his selfishness, left children across the country; and yes, I knew in my gut that I was dealing with a family problem. And yes, we had the same messed up childhood. But we always tried to watch out for each other, we loved each other, and when he shot himself, I was on the other side of the continent. I still feel like I should have been there."

"I understand. He was your only brother. You tried to help each other. Yet, you are adults. Do you believe you are somehow responsible for the decisions he made? That you were responsible for protecting him, the adult, from the abuse that came from your childhood? He made his own decisions."

"When you put it that way . . . as I said I feel like I should have been there!"

"Okay. Our time is up for this session. Next Wednesday, same time?"

Mike hesitated. He knew she was right about Kevin. Still, she was touching a very fragile part of him, an area of guilt that he had placed a wall around since he could remember. Inside that wall was an emptiness, a hole in his soul that he was afraid to fill, too painful even to visit. Dr. Lowell sensed his reticence.

"Mike, I will always do my best to fit you into my schedule when you are ready. Shall I just wait for you to call?"

"No, doctor. No, next Wednesday is fine."

"Good. I'll see you then." She closed the pad she was writing on, stood and walked over to and sat down at her desk. She started writing in what looked like a calendar. Mike gathered himself and as he opened the office door to exit he said, "Thank you."

She gave a slight nod then said, "Good work," and returned to writing. Mike left. He barely remembered walking down the stairs and along the sidewalk. He came to a stop sign and recognized that he needed to pay attention. He had parked somewhere between the doctor's office and his house near Julliard Park. He decided to go and check on his house, since he had been gone for the last few days. His mind was troubled. He wanted to talk more, but Dr. Lowell had made it clear that their time was up.

Lee came to mind, but because she was busy today, he wouldn't be able to see her till tomorrow. He knew he could talk to her. She wouldn't give him therapeutic advice, but she was a good listener. Which made him smile as he thought, *perhaps that's what makes her a good counselor. She did know about the false sighting of my brother a few days ago. I know it was a fluke, yet I chose not to tell Dr. Lowell. I just need to think on it more.* He settled on that last thought for a while. He knew he probably should have talked about it during his session with Dr. Lowell.

He cut down Art Alley toward his house. All looked peaceful and normal, for a major city anyway. He did a general checkup on the house and found himself staring out the kitchen window. He looked out at the park. The homeless man that he helped earlier was gone. He noticed that at the moment there weren't any homeless out there. Which made him reflect, *it should be a crime the way we treat the homeless in this country. Instead, we find ways to make being homeless a crime. It's backassward. As long as the police can arrest the vagabonds and keep them out of the good folks sight, those same people are less afraid.*

"What are you afraid of, crime? I get it. It makes the news! Or are you afraid you're a paystub or two from being like them!" He was commenting to no one and everyone as he talked at the window. "Sure, some of that crime is related to homeless people, but most of that is petty and because of them being homeless. Desperate people make desperate choices. Sometimes we should just lend a helping hand." Mike said this as he stared out at the park, then he shook his head and then said to himself, "I remember a homeless man asking for a buck in front of a store. I gave him a ten and he started crying. As he sobbed, he said to me, 'Thank you for your kindness.'" Then Mike thought, *Imagine how desperate he was that he broke down into tears over a ten-dollar bill. Even so, most of those good folks out there would walk the other way before they gave him even a handful of pocket change.*

Dr. Lowell had watched after Mike closed the door. She knew he wanted to talk more, but she also saw he was in conflict. She had seen this before. A seemingly successful man, successfully hiding his personal torment. Mike was genuinely a good man with a horrible past. He believed he had conquered much of his PTSD because of what he had achieved through his own therapy, but also because of all the self-help books and seminars he did for those who shared the same terrible past. In her mind his seminars and his writing had to be cathartic.

It's clear from his desire to help people afflicted with similar pains that he cares. He told her in their last session that he felt like he was a grown-up version of Holden Caulfield. Except that he wasn't the Catcher in the Rye, but a catcher in their emotional minds. Trying to help them before they fall over the precipice of their wounded selves. Yet his guilt, shame and pain were deeply buried somewhere around the death of his brother.

She opened her computer to look for a psychological concept that would fit Mike. She settled on Reactive Prosocial Behavior, which is a person with PTSD who has a strong desire or drive to help and prevent others from experiencing the same type of pain. She wrote that down and sat back in her chair to think. When you live with so much buried pain for so long, it starts to become part of your day-to-day life. Even to the point where letting it go feels wrong. She thought that maybe that's where Mike had unwittingly settled. His pain was like a bad friend that wouldn't go away so he had to learn to live with this hurt and pained friend. She made a few more notes and then got ready for her next session.

Mike knew what Dr. Lowell was referring to when she brought up his brother's suicide. He knew in his intellectual mind that she was right. As an adult, Kevin was responsible for the choices he made. Yet, just like with that homeless man, sometimes we need to offer a little bit of compassion.

Still, sometimes a genuine desire to help somebody overcome bad life choices can be a wrong choice. Mike believed that the self-centered decisions Kevin made as an adult were because of the inner conflicts directly related to his childhood abuse and his self-abuse. Mike thought about how many times he tried to help his brother. Kevin always nodded in agreement but inevitably went back to the same inappropriate behavior.

When a machine is broken you call a mechanic, but when your spirit is broken it cannot be fixed without the broken human willing to acknowledge the parts that need healing. Mike knew this. He had experienced this. Still, Dr. Lowell's input about his brother's suicide did not feel right. Though, at the moment, he was second-guessing his feelings as well. He made his way to his car and started driving.

As he got closer to the ranch, he started to relax a bit. The kids would be there, and it would be good to see Zeus. He was a good and sweet animal. The thought of seeing the kids made him feel better. He parked his car near the garage. He had a plug-in hybrid. He connected into the charger that Alonzo had mentioned. He saw that there wasn't anybody around. The kids must be off on their own adventure. It was nearly three in the afternoon, so he decided to have a glass of wine. While he sat on the front porch, sipping on a pinot, he thought more about the session with Dr. Lowell.

As he ruminated, Rose and Tyler and their little ones pulled into the driveway. Rose helped Walker get out of her car seat first then gathered Weston. Walker saw Mike and ran over to him. Walker's excitement at everything in her life filled Mike with joy. He loved the way that she loved life. Sometimes she was reticent to jump into an activity with her peers, but he could see her curiosity and at the right time, boom!

She's going to grow up to be a scientist, or like Rose, a really good mom, or better yet, both, Mike thought. As she got closer, that excitement was all over her face.

"Grandpa Mike, we saw a train! Daddy took us to the main station. It was sooo big!"

"Is that right. Wow, you are so lucky. Where did you see it?"

"On the train tracks." She responded in such a way that it should've been obvious to Mike.

"Well, it's a good thing that it was on its tracks."

"We saw the Smart Train at an intersection," Tyler explained. "We weren't too far from Airport Blvd. So, I drove down to the central terminal. There was a place that was open to the public so, we walked around. You gave her a train set for her fourth birthday. Now she wants to see the real trains. We had a fun time, right?" Tyler gently patted Walker's head as he spoke.

"Yeah. They're so big, Grandpa Mike." She stretched out her arms as far as she could. Mike laughed.

"I'm so happy you got to see a real train."

"Yep!"

"Okay, honey, let's get a snack and then maybe we can all take a rest." Rose had a tired baby Weston in her hands. She gently guided Walker into the house.

"Mom, I don't want to take a nap."

"I know. How about an apple?"

"Sure! Can you cut mine into fourthies?" Mike heard Rose laughing as their conversation faded into the house.

"You're a good dad," Mike said to Tyler. Tyler sat down next to Mike.

"Thanks, Mike. You're a good grandpa!" Tyler said with a smile. Mike laughed.

"How are you doing today, Mike?" Tyler became serious.

"I'm okay. Best I can offer at the moment."

"I know you are dealing with some tough stuff. I'm not as knowledgeable as some of the people you know, but I do care and am willing to help in any way that I can."

"Well, let me say, you're a lot smarter than most of the people I know. Which I think you know as well. Thank you for taking such good care of Rose and your kids. A lot of what I'm going through is because we as kids were badly abused. That, apparently, takes a lifetime of healing. I did my best to make sure my girls were protected and well loved. It's clear that you are doing the same for yours."

"Thank you, Mike."

"Yeah, broken people beget broken people. My two sisters and I, after Kevin's death, made a commitment, a promise to each other, that we would end that pattern of broken kids. I think we succeeded. You came from a family that deeply cares for each other. It shows. One of the issues about coming from such broken place is that as an adult its trauma haunts you from a distant past. So, I'm dealing with something that happened so many years ago. It's on me to deal with stuff that I never had any control over. Even if you reach a point where you think, 'I'm healed,' you're really not. The survivors, like me, and in order to survive, have learned to accept love, to give love, to love the self, but there are triggers, and they can sometimes be devastating. Still, when I'm in such a place, my family, my friends are a haven. So, thank you for being an important part of this haven."

"Well, we can see that you have been triggered, as you say. Know that we are here for you if we can help."

"Thank you, Tyler."

"Are you here for dinner?"

"Yes, I will be. Let me cook tonight. Shall we have a tri-tip?"

"That sounds great. But, if you don't mind, I'll cook it on the

BBQ."

"I don't. Sounds good," Mike said with a smile.

"Cool. I'm going to go lay down with the fam."

"Okay. I'll head into town and grab us the tri-tip."

"Hmm, grab a couple of four packs too."

"Will do. And thanks again Tyler." Tyler nodded and headed into the house. Mike watched him, and not for the last time thought, *He's a good man,* as he made his way to his car.

CHAPTER TEN

"Dad, we have eight adults and one toddler that we need to seat. I think we need a bigger table," Rose said as she looked from the kitchen into the dining/living room area.

"Yeah . . . Perhaps we can sit you guys around the coffee table. Though that leaves six adults to try and fit around this kitchen table."

"Or we could use the kitchen table as a launch pad." Rose pointed at the small round table.

"A what?"

"We could set all the prepared food on this table, and then add a card table to the long table on the back porch and that way everybody sits together." She said it as if it were obvious.

"Okay, good idea."

That was early Thursday. Mike was in good spirits. He'd slept well. No nightmares Wednesday night, for which he was grateful. Rose was taking charge of the Friday dinner preparations. Tyler was in the living room watching a kids' show with Walker. Weston was deep asleep on a quilt. Sarah was still upstairs.

"Okay, we've been talking, here and there, about what we are planning for dinner, but now we need to settle on the menu." Rose grabbed a notepad and walked into the living room.

"Sounds good. All I know is that I'm on BBQ duty," Tyler interjected.

"Wouldn't have it any other way." Rose laughed. Mike smiled. The familial banter between the two of them showed how much they cared for each other.

"I'm gonna help Daddy!" Walker made it clear that she was part of the decision making.

“Couldn’t do it without you, little one.” Tyler gave her a hug. She loved her Daddy.

“Okay, let’s plan this.” Rose sat where she could see them and plopped a pad on the coffee table.

That’s how Thursday started and for the most part ended. They got most of their shopping done and by the end of the day Mike did get to spend some time with Lee. Walker had to hear Twinkle Twinkle Little Star on the piano one more time, but eventually Lee and Mike sat and talked on the back porch. Somewhere in their conversations the last session with Dr. Lowell came up.

“It’s not like I was disagreeing that my brother was responsible for his own decisions. I get that intellectually. It’s just that I don’t think things are that black and white.”

“Of course, things are not just black and white, Mike. So, based on what you’ve told me, plus the fact that Dr. Lowell is working EMDR with you, and based on your last meeting, I would say that she is looking at helping you from a bottom-up perspective. Which makes sense to me. Something is triggering you. I would say that she’s looking for a base that the two of you can use to launch some healing.

“She has postulated, and you agree, that Kevin, as an adult, made his own decisions. If I may suggest, which you should talk with your therapist, consider that you may want to work more on your acceptance. I am familiar with Dr. Lowell. She is a professional. If you could accept her premise that you are not responsible for Kevin’s decisions, I think it may be helpful. And please, I am not offering therapeutic advice. I am suggesting you open yourself to her input a bit more. And yes, this is me talking from my experience as a counselor.”

“I appreciate your advice, Lee. I always do.”

They talked for about another hour. It was getting late so Lee decided it was time to head home. Mike walked her to her car. After they said their goodnights, Mike made his way back into the main house. The kids were in bed, though Mike could hear Weston fussing a bit. Mike did the usual check on lights and locks and eventually made his way into bed. That night Mike had another nightmare.

This time he was the adult in a dark room. There was a door to one side that was partially open. Through the door's opening he could see stairs leading up to what he believed to be an attic. Even as the adult in his dream there was still an ever-present feeling of danger and fear. The darkness surrounded him like a blanket, but as an adult it wasn't covering his head.

He could see and move as he wished. He looked at the door and knew there was something not right with it. It reminded him of the time at his grandmother's house, but this time he was in charge. Though it was scary, he felt a need to go up those stairs. He did. When he reached the top there seemed to be some light there, but it faintly lit the space.

There were two items in the attic room. Where the roof angled down to his left there was something that looked like a small bed. He couldn't be sure because the bed and another adult near the bed were shaded and dark. He knew this was the nightmare. As that thought filled his dream mind the darkened adult started moving toward him. Mike's anger at the shadow figure grew intensely. He prepared himself to meet that darkened abuser. As he physically set himself to fight, he woke up.

Mike, as a side sleeper now awake, rolled onto his back. His mind went through the details of the dream. He was ready to violently defend himself against that shadow figure. Still, the fear was also there. Maybe that's why he popped out of the dream.

Enough of these nightmares. At least I was the adult in this one, he thought. As he lay there he also thought about the familiarity of a doorway to an attic. The haunted memory from his grandmother's house of that evening, so many years ago; the bed, the door and the sad clown at the top of the stairs rolled around the back of his mind. The thought of his brother took over. *It's interesting how the memory of my brother haunts me as much as the childhood abuse.*

It was still dark out. There was no clock, and he didn't reach for his phone. Whatever the time, he knew he needed to get back to sleep. Eventually he did.

He slept later than usual. He woke to the sounds of Walker running around the house. Rose was trying to hush her daughter. It worked for about one minute and then she was all excited again, running through the long hallway. She was ready to help with the family gathering. Mike thought about last night's dream as he got dressed. It was the first time that, while his mind slipped into the recurring nightmares from his childhood abuse, he was solely the adult. He had morphed from the fearful child into an adult in previous dreams, but this time he was his age. The fear was there, but the child was not. That was something to think about.

He made his way out to the kitchen. Tyler had whipped up some scrambled eggs and a platter of bacon. A new pot of coffee was brewing. Rose was in the living room area nursing Weston. Sarah was sipping her coffee and entertaining Walker.

"Coffee will be ready in a few minutes. Eggs and bacon are by the stove. Please help yourself," Tyler said to Mike.

"Dad, what time is Lee going to be here?" It was Sarah.

"Around one. What about Elizabeth?"

"She said around the same time. I think Mom and Bill will be here to help around noon."

"Great. You sent them the gate code?"

"Yes, and also Elizabeth."

"Yes. Good."

"Miss Lee is going to be here today?" Walker stood up from the game she and Sarah were playing.

"Yes, honey, she is."

"I want to hear the Little Star song again!" Walker exclaimed.

"Pretty soon you'll be playing it for us," Rose said as she smiled at her daughter.

"I'll show you now." Walker ran over to the piano and started playing. It was a bit of a cacophony.

"Thanks, Dad. I guess I'm going to have to get a practice piano and some lessons now," Rose said as she put Weston on the floor.

"Hey, you never know," Mike replied with a shrug.

The morning flowed. Everybody was busy. Rose suddenly remembered forgotten dinner items, sending Tyler zipping off to the nearest store. There was lots of family banter, and when Tyler returned from the store, he and Walker played ball with Zeus. Somewhere around noon Tyler started cooking. Virginia and Bill arrived. They all helped Sarah and Rose prepare for the gathering. Walker and Mike were telling jokes on the front porch.

"Knock-knock, Grandpa Mike." Walker had a great joke in mind.

"Who's there?" Mike played along.

"Under there." She said as she giggled. Mike knew what was coming.

"Under where?"

"You said underwear!" Walker shouted as she laughed and giggled. Mike laughed along with her. She was a happy little one. She ran to her daddy who was cooking out on the creek side porch.

"Daddy, Grandpa Mike said underwear." Tyler laughed. He had heard that joke before.

"Mike, did you say underwear to my daughter?" Tyler yelled. Mike heard laughter from the kitchen as they all knew the joke.

"Guilty as charged," Mike yelled back.

"Okay, Grandpa, it's your turn to tell me a joke." Walker had scooted around the side of the house and back to the front porch with Mike. She jumped up on the seat next to her grandpa.

"Let me think." Mike ran his fingers across his chin as he pretended to be deep in thought.

"Hmm, hmm." Then he stopped. As he was pretend thinking he saw something that startled him. Across the yard and near the bridge that led to the trails into the hills stood a young man. Just like the incident at the store a few days ago, this person looked like his brother.

"Hey." Mike yelled as he stood. The young man looked at him but did not move.

"Hey." Mike yelled again.

"Grandpa Mike?" Walker stood next to Mike, reaching for his hand. Mike could see her concern. Adults yelling can be scary.

"Walker, I need you to go into the house and help your mom and dad. Okay?"

"Why, Grandpa?"

"It's okay, honey. Just go inside and help." Mike ushered her through the front door and assured her one more time before he closed the door. "Be a big girl and help." Mike closed the door and spun around. Walker watched through the glass door as Mike turned and said aloud, "I know you're not Kevin." Then he yelled, "Who are you?" He ran toward the bridge and the paths that led into the hills.

Walker looked at where he was running and then out near the bridge. There was nobody there. Like most children near her age, close to five, she was more aware of the world than adults gave her credit for. She knew her grandfather was upset. She didn't know why. At first, she thought that she had done something wrong, then she remembered they were playing jokes with each other. Maybe this was a joke. She smiled. She walked by the piano and ran her fingers over a few keys. Then she heard her dad say, "Tri-tips will be done in about forty minutes."

After Mike ushered Walker into the house, he spun and started to run toward the man he saw, except he was no longer there. He thought about calling for Tyler.

"What the hell… he's not my brother. I've got this." he said to himself as he ran. He made it to the bridge and stopped. The young man was nowhere to be seen. "Hey!" Mike yelled again. He took a quick look back at the main house, then crossed the bridge into the trails.

There were many to choose from. He decided to follow the trail that led up to an aquifer that supplied the drinking water for the house. A couple of times he stopped and yelled, "Hey, hello!" There was no response. He continued up the trail and then off to the left. Eventually he came to a clearing with an old, burnt-out redwood tree stump.

This was once a favorite spot of Mike's. Over the years he kept it clear of excess growth and was happy to see that Alonzo did the same. He stopped and stood near the old stump. Like many of the ancient redwood remnants the center was a bit hollowed out. His daughter, Sarah, when she was around seven, used to climb in the center of the stump and pretended it was a boat. A lot of memories created here. There was an opening on the side facing the clearing that was a good spot to sit. He gave a half-hearted, "Hey, hello!" one more time and then sat in the old familiar place to think.

It felt like the universe was playing a game with him. He looked around and thought about the odd couple of appearances of his brother. Was his mind playing tricks? He shook his head as the nightmares came into his mind. The lifelong feelings of grief, pain, guilt and anger started to spin in his stomach and mind. The mistakes he made. The things he could have done differently. The strange and coincidental encounters recently. His brother. His brother. His brother. His brother. He missed Kevin.

"I guess I should head back," he murmured to himself. As he got ready to rise something caught his eye. He picked it up. It was an old tiny keepsake picture frame. It clearly had been there for some time. He did his best to brush away the caked dirt. There was a photo behind a cracked glass cover. He couldn't get all the dirt away and, curious to see what the photo was, he managed to pull off the back clips holding the old picture. When he looked at it, it brought tears to his eyes. It was a photo of his brother with Sarah on his lap that Mike had taken when she was nearly four. They were sitting on a large whalebone in front of an inn in the town of Bodega Bay. They both wore big smiles.

He remembered that photo. It was about a year before Kevin took his life. Mike studied the photo. He shook his head as he thought about the years Kevin and he spent in their youth. They were inseparable. He studied the photo while he thought, *what is going on?*

Then he felt it. That feeling as if someone or something was watching him. He looked forward and to the right. Nothing. He looked to his left and there it was. The mountain lion that had sat by the fence and watched him a week or so ago. The lion was no more than twenty feet away, standing and looking at Mike. The big cat was swishing his tail, which did make Mike a little nervous.

He calmly looked at either side of him to see if there was a stick or something he could pick up. These animals usually won't mess with a human with something big in their hands. There was nothing close. He looked back at the mountain lion. The animal seemed to be curious. He was just standing still and staring at Mike. He could feel that the cat was no threat.

"You know, it's a bit odd that you're here where I can see you." The cat stood still and continued to watch Mike.

"Are you just inquisitive?"

This time the lion gave a low raspy meow. Like it was trying to say something to Mike.

"Did you know another human at some time? You seem very comfortable just staring at me."

Again, the cat gave a raspy response. It was almost like a low, non-threatening growl mixed with a cat's meow. It was weird. Still, Mike did not feel in danger. For a second Mike thought he would approach the animal, but then, gave in to common sense. A mountain lion is a dangerous predator. Mike decided it was best to stay put, for now.

"This is one of the more interesting mountain lion sightings I've ever seen." The man's voice startled both the cat and Mike. The cat suddenly became tense. He looked in the direction of the man's voice. He then looked back at Mike. He gave another low raspy cat growl and then sprang into the forest. Mike listened to the cat's soft feet pat the ground as it ran away. Then he looked back at the newcomer. When it became clear who the man was Mike stood, jaw down and just stared. It was the man in white.

"Do you and that lion have some sort of detente going on?" The man in white asked with a slight smile.

Mike stared. The man wasn't completely in white. He was wearing a white polo top but this time he was in blue jeans. He still was wearing the white bucket hat that Mike had seen before.

"Who are you? What are you doing here?" Mike finally managed to speak.

"Sorry, my name is Angelo. We kind of met a few years ago. I was at the edge of the winery, just over there. I heard you yelling, "Hey, Hello'. I thought someone might need help, so I came to check."

"You're that man I saw on the street and in the store. I had this feeling I needed to connect with you, but each time I tried, you were gone. We kind of met?"

"Yes. I attended a couple of your seminars in Phoenix. Spiritually, I wasn't in a good place. I was profoundly affected by your courage and confidence to talk about your past. How it wreaked havoc in your life, and about all the work you did to put it behind you, or not let it control you. That animal seemed very comfortable just watching you. Have you met it before?"

"Yes, a week or so ago it sat next to the fence by the house entrance. I was sitting on the front porch, and just like now, it simply watched me. I was a bit unnerved by the encounter, but I wasn't afraid. It was like it wanted to meet, but we both, wisely, kept our distance."

"Hmm, maybe it's your spirit animal."

"Interesting."

"Well, you wrote about it. There are things, events, that as humans we can't explain, or have lost our ability to understand. That ability is there; we just don't listen to our intuition. As Einstein said, 'The intuitive mind is a sacred gift, and the rational mind is a faithful servant. We have created a society that honors the servant and has forgotten the gift.'

"Some primitive parts of us are still connected to our planet and the life around us, as you wrote in one of your books. The times you knew that someone, or something, was going to fall, and they did. You wrote about knowing your brother had just shot himself, even though you were 3000 miles away. And how is it that we know when someone is looking at us?" As Angelo spoke, he meandered closer to Mike.

"Yes." Mike gave a small nod as he looked back to where the lion had jumped into the forest.

"Do you think that cat will be back?" They were closer to the center of the clearing.

"No. Funny, that feels certain." Mike looked again. There were a few seconds of awkward silence then Angelo spoke.

"I lost my sister. She wasn't carrying the transgenerational cycle of abuse, like your brother, but she never recovered from her childhood sexual assault. She was taking opioids just to survive. One day she gave up and crammed a bottle of them down her throat. That was about a month before I first attended your seminar." Angelo looked away into the past as he talked about his sister's death. He shook his head and went quiet.

"I know your pain." Mike touched Angelo's shoulder.

"I know. I remember you talking about your brother. This is really a cool spot." Angelo gestured about the clearing and the redwood stump. He took a step then stopped. "I was in a bad place when I came to see you. I am grateful for your wisdom and insight into what we, as survivors, go through. You may not remember, but we talked after the second seminar that I attended. You strongly encouraged therapy. I was lucky. I found a great therapist. I found a way to understand my sister's decision. Still, it hurts, but I can forgive her for the pain she left inside me. I know she's in a better place." He stopped and looked at Mike, "That's the reason I'm here."

"Because of your sister?"

"As I learned not to take her death personally, I also learned a great deal about me. I'll always remember how confident you looked as you spoke about your abusive history. How you were able to put self-blame and guilt and more under your control as an adult and not be dominated by the PTSD caused by the abusive past. I wanted that. That self-confidence. It took me a while, though I am still learning."

"Hopefully we never stop learning."

"Yes. But like you I could feel things that were not explainable. Things that I either ignored or denied for most of my life. They are the gut feelings that make up a big part of who I am. I embrace those feelings now. Like you I have learned how to accept who I am. To be me, in all situations. I don't let myself be influenced by other people's opinions, ideologies, anything that someone may use to try to hold power over me or control the way I think. I am, for the first time in my life, me. And a big part of me is those 'feelings' that I sometimes get. I don't understand where they come from, but I trust them. So far, they have always been right. There's a term for them that has just escaped my brain."

"Interoception."

"What?"

"Interoception is one of the descriptive words you are looking for. Sometimes it's called the seventh sense. Another is cryptaesthesia. This refers to our so-called sixth sense. The ability to gain or receive information with our minds. A so-called form of ESP, a part of our intuition. You were saying you're here because of your sister?"

"No. I am here because of your brother." Angelo looked straight at Mike as he said that. All of Mike's internal guards went up. As he started to say something Angelo put up his hand, quieting Mike. He continued, "About four weeks ago, just before I was on this trip to the wine country with some friends, I started having these feelings about my sister. The feelings were such that I knew she was in a better place. That she was happy. That she was sorry for the pain she left behind with me. Then something happened. I started to have these very strong feelings about your brother. It was like my sister was some sort of a liaison. Those feelings were very strong. So strong I felt overwhelmed."

"My brother?"

"Yes."

"What are you talking about? What do you mean, feelings?"

"Feelings that I could only identify as coming from your brother, Kevin. These feelings were of deep sorrow. So much so, that I became depressed and tried to shut them out. He wouldn't let me. Then I decided to try to open my mind during meditation. Again, the feeling of sorrow was profuse."

"He had a rough life."

"Let me finish. Because what else came through to me was regret. Finally, I decided to open myself to as much as I could receive, and what I felt was a river of sorrow and regret. That is where I was when we first stood across from each other on that street corner. I knew I had a message for you, but it wasn't complete. Something told me to wait. I am sorry for ghosting you these last few weeks. The timing wasn't right."

"I think I understand. I've been in a painful place over my brother for a long time. There have been better days, but recently it's been tough."

"I know. Your brother has seen or felt that. It finally came to me in a burst of clarity. Your brother's sorrow and regret are not so much for his time among the living, though he certainly has experienced that, no, right now, what I am experiencing from him is for you."

"Me!"

"Yes. Kevin is reaching out through me to tell you to stop."

"Stop?"

"Yes, stop. You feel regret, guilt and pain over not being there when he took his life. And all those negative feelings because you believe you could've somehow helped him, stopped him. No, it was his decision. And yes, I have experienced those feelings of grief and of 'what could I have done,' and the internal pain, these are all normal for those of us who still walk the Earth after a loved one has left us behind. But, for us, the abused, we who were damaged by those who were supposed to take care of us, that type of pain and guilt feels worse. Sadly, we wear that trauma. There are times when we are okay, yet, we are also, and often without any warning, easily triggered.

"Kevin is in a better place. He wants you to know as an adult he made his decision, all his own decisions. He wants you to know that he loves you. He's always loved you. He wants you to drop your guilt.

"He will wander among the stars forever regretting the lies and pain he caused to, not only his family, but to almost everyone he met. He wishes for you to let go of your pain and guilt around his death. Even though you may not feel it, it had nothing to do with you."

"I know that intellectually, but—"

"Forgive me for interrupting. These feelings are strong. I believe you have an intuitive mind as well. Why Kevin has not been able to touch you, I don't know. But sometimes it's best to accept an event as opposed to try to push it away. Not only is your brother wishing you to let him go, but he's also afraid you might be holding him too hard. I don't pretend to make sense on how I can receive these types of feelings, but I have learned to accept this part of who I am. Perhaps you just need to learn to accept that Kevin is in one place and you are here. It feels like he really wants you to let him go."

"That's the second time in two days I have been told that I should learn to accept."

"You're a good man, Mike. That's something else I felt from your brother, he's proud of you. I'm grateful for you. I listen to people talk after your seminars. People love you, Mike. They are moved, in the right direction, to help themselves. You have helped so many. Thank you." Angelo reached out with his right hand to shake with Mike. Mike hesitated a couple of seconds before he shook Angelo's hand. It was warm. When Mike touched Angelo's hand his whole body felt lighter. Maybe it was just in his mind. There was much to think about.

"Well, today you have helped me. Thank you," Mike said sincerely.

"I feel like a burden has been lifted from my shoulders. I know you not to be a religious man, but I believe you to be a spiritual being, I hope you can accept what I have been tasked to share with you."

"I can. And again, thank you. I will make more of a positive effort. If you should hear from my brother again, would you tell him I love him."

"I think he knows."

"Dad!" It was Sarah's voice in the distance.

"Well, you're being paged and I need to get back. Again, thank you, Mike." Angelo shook Mike's hand again and turned back toward the neighboring winery.

Mike took a second to look at his hand and then watched Angelo turn a corner and then he was gone. Mike looked at the empty trail and thought about what had just happened. Then his brother came to mind. As the mist in his eyes grew, he made his way back to the redwood stump and sat down. He sank his forehead into his hands and thought, *Okay, it's time to accept. I love you brother, but I am going to make an effort to let all this Earthly pain and guilt go. Be at peace and I will do my best to be the same here.* He sat there, head in hands, and let the conversation with Angelo sink into his mind, into his soul. Then he felt something lick his hands. Startled, thinking it was the mountain lion, he looked up. It was Zeus.

"Dad!" Again it was from Sarah.

Walker had watched as Mike ran into the forest. The adults were laughing and over-talking as they were getting the porch and the serving tables ready. Rose was just coming back from checking on the baby and Walker, now at the piano, was tapping different keys. Rose encouraged Walker to play quietly when there was a knock at the door. She could see through the glass that Lee had arrived.

"Walker, do you want to let Lee in?"

"Yeah, she can show me the Twinkle Star song again." She ran to the door followed by Rose.

"Hi, Lee. I'm so glad you're here," Rose said as she gave Lee a hug.

"Same."

"Twinkle Twinkle." Walker exclaimed. She grabbed Lee's hand to lead her to the piano.

"Honey, let her get settled. She can show you after she says hi to Grandpa. Hey, Dad." Rose said as she moved toward the front porch. No answer.

"Hmm . . . I'll check the side porch."

"That's all right. I'll find him." Lee said.

"He went off to the bridge," Walker said, trying to be helpful.

"He went where?" Rose asked.

"To the bridge. I saw him run that way. We were on the porch telling jokes and he saw somebody by the bridge. He told me to go into the house and help. Then he ran," Walker said and pointed at the same time.

"Oh, did he say anything else?" Rose shrugged and looked apologetically at Lee.

"Hi Lee." Sarah walked in from the kitchen to give her a hug. "I hope you're hungry."

"He said something about Kevin and then ran to the bridge." Walker said to her mom. That stopped all three adults.

"Who said something about Kevin?" Sarah became serious.

"Grandpa. He put me in the house and said . . . I don't remember . . . something about Kevin." Walker could see the adults' concern.

"Then what happened?" Rose asked.

"And then he ran to the bridge."

"He mentioned Kevin?" This time it was Lee. Walker nodded her head. Lee looked at the two girls and said, "I think we should go find him."

"Tyler!" Rose shouted through the doorway out to where he was grilling.

"Yeah, babe?"

"You've got Walker. Honey, go to daddy."

"No, I wanna help."

"Honey–"

"Mom, I wanna help find grandpa."

"Okay. Ty, never mind, she's with me. You need to stay next to me, understand."

"I know, Mom."

"There are ticks, rattlesnakes and a mountain lion out there. You stay with me, clear."

"Yes, Mom." Rose, Lee and Walker were the first out the door.

"Hey you guys, Elizabeth may show up while we're gone. Tell her I'll be right back, please." Sarah yelled back at her mom and Bill as she walked out. She caught up with Rose and Lee. "There are some walking sticks next to the bridge. We should split up. I think Lee and I should go up and off to the left and Rose, you and Walker to the right."

"Okay, sounds good." Just then Zeus came running up with them. He loved running through the forest.

"Good boy, Zeus. We're going to check on Dad. Go git 'im." Rose said to the dog as they crossed the bridge. Because he liked to run through the brush, Rose thought he could help. She and Walker went off to the right. Zeus bolted up and to the left, followed by Sarah and Lee.

Mike was relieved that it wasn't the lion licking his hands. Zeus was clearly happy to see him. "You're a good boy," Mike said to the dog as he scratched and rubbed around Zeus' ears.

"Dad!" Again, he heard Sarah's call.

"Up here." He yelled in the direction of Sarah's voice. "At the clearing where the old tree stump is." He stood up and along with Zeus started on the trail that led back to the house. He turned back toward the clearing and smiled.

Something extraordinary had just happened. His chance meeting with Angelo was magical. It was cathartic. He felt like he'd just had one of the best therapy sessions ever. He felt much lighter and clearer. He thought about Kevin. "I miss you, brother. I still think it would have been different, for all of us kids, if we'd had a better childhood. And I can and will let you go. Love you." He took a couple more seconds to look at the clearing, then turned and started back.

"Dad!" Sarah ran up and stopped him. She held his arms and peered deep into his eyes. "Are you all right? Why are you up here? Walker overheard you, what were you saying about Kevin?"

"I am fine. Walker's a good kid. I'm up here because I seem to have needed a meeting with the universe."

"What? The universe? What does that mean? And Kevin? Dad, I'm concerned."

"I see that sweetheart. Let me explain."

"Hey you, what's going on? Are you all right?" Lee caught up with the two of them.

"I'm fine. I was telling my daughter, I seem to have been in need of a meeting with the universe. I met the man in white." Mike gestured to Sarah as he said the last sentence.

"The man in white? Did you think he was Kevin?" Sarah always liked clarity.

"No, that's something else. His name is Angelo and he attended a couple of my seminars. He wanted to thank me for helping him, and others. He is also one of those unique people who can feel things with his mind as well as the other five senses."

"What does that mean?" It was Lee.

"He lost his sister to suicide . . .Like Kevin. Anyway, in a certain psychic, or maybe spiritual incident he could feel his sister wanting him to let her go. He was holding on to her with his guilt, pain and remorse. During that enlightened experience with her, he felt strong and similar feelings about my brother. So strong it took him until recently to understand what Kevin was trying to reveal to him.

"Lee, you and Dr. Lowell have encouraged me to accept that there was nothing I could have done to help Kevin. His choices were his choices. And as much as that hurts I think I have reached a point where I can forgive him for the pain he left in my heart when he killed himself. And I can forgive me for those same feelings. I think I can let him go and move on knowing he's where he's supposed to be. So, through seeing Angelo, and what he had to share, is what I mean when I say I had a meeting with the universe. We all know there are moments that we experience which are unexplainable. We all have had, at different times, experienced those types of inexplicable feelings."

"Dad, Kevin?" Sarah was insistent.

"The young man that I saw near our bridge looked like him. I knew he wasn't Kevin. Walker heard me mention Kevin, but what she didn't hear was that I also said, 'I know you're not my brother'. But I had to run after him. Sarah, as you pointed out, Kevin is dead. I know that. But as I saw that young man, I had to know. In my mind and heart, I needed to have an answer to what is happening with me. I know I'm not hallucinating. What I saw was real. Still, something tied to my feelings these past few weeks, motivated me to find an answer. I thought maybe that young man."

"Did you find him?" Lee asked.

"No."

"Do you find that interesting?"

"Funnily, no. Given this interaction with Angelo, I'm going to just accept it's something that I can't explain but am grateful to have experienced."

"Dad!" The three of them heard the call in the distance.

"That's Rose and Walker looking for you," Sarah said.

"We should let her know we found Mike," Lee said.

"Yeah, I'll run down and tell her."

"Actually, Sarah, you should walk your dad back. I'll scoot down to the other trail and let her know."

"You sure?"

"Yeah, see you at the house." Lee did a fast walk down the trail to find Rose and Walker.

"You know, Dad, she likes you." Sarah said after thay had walked in silence for a few minutes.

"Oh, I know. We have been friends for a long time. I like her too."

"Yes, but Dad, she really likes you."

"Ueah, but we're just sweet friends."

"No, Dad, she really, really likes you."

"Oh, you mean..."

"Yeah. You should encourage her."

"We've been friends for so long I never wanted to push us into something that would make her uncomfortable."

"I get it. But as a woman I also see where you two could be closer. If you know what I mean."

"Oh, yes, okay. Thanks."

"Love you. Ah, the bridge."

Sarah and Mike waited on the other side of the bridge for Rose, Walker and Lee. Rose had questions for Mike but was satisfied with his responses. They made their way to the house and after entering were cornered by the girl's mom and Bill and Elizabeth. All from a place of love and caring. After emotions settled, Walker convinced Lee to play Twinkle Twinkle Little Star again. Afterward Walker's song was over Lee started plucking on the piano then suddenly went into a song that Mike's kids knew.

"Dad, she's playing that song that you always tear up to," Rose said with a big smile.

"What?" Mike made his way to the piano.

"It's 'North', by Sleeping at Last." Sarah said.

Everybody listened to Lee's rendition of such a beautiful song and as the last hook was played they all sang:

> Give us bread
> Give us salt
> Give us wine.

"Nice." Elizabeth spoke first.

"Yeah, I do love that song," Mike said to Lee. She nodded.

"I do know you," she said with a smile.

"Oh, shoot, I'm pretty sure the meat is ready," Tyler said as he quickly headed back out to the grill.

"Okay, let's get this family gathering going. What can I do to help?" Mike asked Rose.

"Well, help me get the serving table set." Mike followed her into the kitchen. She started giving tasks to different people. Tyler came rushing in looking for a large dish to plate the meat. Virginia and Bill were making final preparations on the dinner table. Sarah and Elizabeth were near the stove, laughing. It was organized chaos. Mike looked around with a big smile. Suddenly he could hear Walker at the piano. He looked back toward the piano room; Lee was showing Walker how to play her song one key at a time. Mike continued to look around. His eyes grew a little misty as he thought, *this is what love looks like. Thank you, Angelo.*

"Oh, look. Dad's getting emotional again." Rose said with a big smile. "C'mon everybody. Let's eat."

There was some general chitchat and big smiles as they all congregated around the serving table. Though Mike was smiling and laughing with the family, he was still thinking about his conversation with Angelo. In his heart he felt cleansed. Then he remembered that he was the adult in his last bad dream. Both things made him smile. He could feel it; there were some good days ahead.

The End (or a new beginning)

THE SECRET DRAGON

In the summer hazy memories of my youth
We were knights, you and I. Both
With mighty wooden swords riding on
Broom-handle steeds with fiery bottle-cap-eyes.
We'd gallop and explore
The undiscovered trails,
To the vacant lots next door.

There we slayed the bad and
Saved the good.
We were the stuff of legends,
You and I.

On our street
We climbed the highest hill,
And rode our giant cardboard ships,
Like two captains on a stormy sea,
Screaming down the precipice,
Till we fell
And rolled
In an entangled clump of laughter and glee.
And never satisfied we climbed to the top
Only to scuttle down
Again and again.

On our street were
Winter castles of newly fallen snow;
Shining sparkling fortresses,
Built by the two of us,

The hero knights,
Armed with snowballs,
Standing back to back,
Surrounded by enemies,
Too scared to attack.

On our street
We were the heroes,
You and I. Yet

On our street lived
A secret dragon.

She would visit us,
In the night.
Her sharp and crooked claws
Reaching down,
Pressing,
Smothering
The fear,
The screams
That nobody heard,
Or chose not to hear.
Ripping away
Trust and tears
Leaving only a
Piece of flesh,
Betrayal and
Nightmares.
She was the dragon.

She was family,
Yet,
When we saw her
We
Would
RUN!

. . . if we could.

When we did escape
To some secret place,
Like heroes need to do,
We ran, stumbling, through the conquered fence
To the imaginal lands a yard away.

There in our secret hide-a-way tree,
Where we flew like monkeys,
Devouring the ripe, juicy, grapes
That hung in easy reach of
Our greedy little fingers;
Our mumbling mouths,
Filled till they spilled,
Running purple down our chins.
There in that
Safe and sacred spot
We'd howl at the skies,
But never talk
Of the dragon we couldn't slay.

In our safe spot
We were the heroes,
My brother,
You and I.

Time passed.
The hero-child faded,
Left behind with forgotten toys
And stolen innocence.
Gone were the knights.
Grown were the diffident courtiers, and
Three thousand miles apart,
You reached out and
I wasn't there.

You cried pitiful tears
Caused by those painful years, and
I wasn't there.
The wooden steed stood
Standing alone in the corner of your kitchen,
Lamenting the loss of the hero child and
I wasn't there.

But the dragon was . . .

Your final scream at heaven
Was a howl for peace.

So, it is
You are there
And I am here.

www.ingramcontent.com/pod-product-compliance
Lightning Source LLC
LaVergne TN
LVHW011029110826
845149LV00015B/3351

* 9 7 9 8 9 9 9 6 7 2 1 4 8 *